Mauritius [illegible] Looking Glass: A Collection of Short Stories

by

Sir Satcam Boolell

The Pentland Press Limited
Edinburgh · Cambridge · Durham · USA

First published in 2000 by
The Pentland Press Ltd.
1 Hutton Close
South Church
Bishop Auckland
Durham

British Library Cataloguing in Publication Data.
A catalogue record for this book is available
from the British Library.

ISBN 1 85821 755 5

Typeset by George Wishart & Associates, Whitley Bay.
Printed and bound by Antony Rowe Ltd., Chippenham.

~ Acknowledgements ~

I wish to express my deep appreciation to Mr Mahmood Tally, formerly Mauritius Ambassador to Cairo, for his valuable criticism; to Mrs Dolores Ditner, Director, Language Centre, University College London, for her patience in reading the manuscripts and suggesting several corrections; and finally to my wife, Myrtha, for sustaining me in my efforts to write the stories.

~ Contents ~

~ Foreword ~

This collection of stories will delight any prospective visitor to Mauritius or anyone interested in gaining an insight into its people's cultural heritage.

Hindus, Muslims, Chinese, Europeans – all living alongside each other in a harmony which would surprise the average tourist; these stories vividly portray the traditional values inherent to the Mauritian way of life and although Sir Satcam laments the social consequences of a certain level of industrialisation, Mauritian society still remains an example to most of us.

I am sure you will enjoy reading these stories as much as I did and that having done so, your visit to this beautiful country will be enriched by the background knowledge thus acquired of these islanders whose charm, sense of welcome and friendliness will contribute to making your visit so memorable.

Dolorès Ditner
University College London

~ Introduction ~

Mauritius, a small island in the Indian Ocean, off the east coast of Madagascar, is a mosaic of races and cultures. Colonized by the French in the early eighteenth century, the island is home today to the descendants of French, African slaves, Indian indentured labourers and Chinese traders and coolies. The cohabitation of these diverse elements over the years has had the salutary effect of removing many cultural and religious prejudices. The spirit of understanding and tolerance which developed has forged a society which evokes the admiration of visitors from the unsettled regions of the world. Ever since Independence, a pride in a common belongingness and an ambition for nationhood are gradually encouraging the emergence of a definable national identity.

The continuation of the colonial policy of granting total freedom for the preservation and expansion of ancestral values in their diverse manifestations has been a great contributory factor in holding together the social fabric and keeping at bay any fissiparous tendency. An educational system which makes it compulsory for all children to follow the same curriculum and sit on the same bench under the tutelage of the same teacher has strengthened the feeling from an early age that a common destiny presides over the future of all the citizens of Mauritius.

But human beings, wherever they are and whatever the era they live in, are subjected to the same vexations in their daily life.

I have tried in this collection to give an insight into the daily struggles of two Indian families for whom certain values could only be sacrificed at the risk of social ostracism. It is true that the Indians have come a long way from the early thirties when the stories took place. But the battle is not yet over, it still continues.

The Story of the Chinese Shopkeeper is designed to mark a watershed in the attitude of the young educated class, not only of Indians but of other ethnic groups as well, in regard to inter-racial and inter-religious matrimonial alliances. Such alliances are no longer frowned upon, they are accepted, although not encouraged. There was a time when such unions would have provoked a small riot with the girl's family taking up arms to prevent what was considered a disgrace. Those days are gone and even orthodox parents bow to the inevitable consequence of a mixed society.

The story of *Gaston* carries a special message and is an answer to the harm which the protagonists of exclusion are doing to the delicate fabric of Mauritian society. The theory that a section of the population, by virtue of their ethnic background, is neglected and excluded from the beneficial effects of development is without foundation. Mauritius is one of those countries where equal opportunities for education and economic advancement are made available to one and all without distinction of colour or creed. Every individual has the potential to rise above the station to which they belong: they must only have the ambition and the determination to achieve it. Among the people designated as being excluded are highly skilled masons, carpenters and mechanics. Their earnings could not be inferior to those of manual workers of other ethnic groups; if anything, they are far superior. Most of them have benefited from housing on generous terms. Industries, which are located near their settlement, provide advantageous opportunities for employment. Where is the problem then? The problem is self-inflicted. Instead of the exclusion ghetto, they should be taught the way to improvement, by investing in their children's education and giving them a stable social environment. Gaston and his grandson, Ernest, are the role models which they could copy.

The Temple in the Sea brings us closer to modern Mauritius, the discovery of which by foreign tourists has opened up a new chapter in our economy. Gone are the days when employment in the sugar industry was the only hope for the large multitude of job seekers. Post independent Mauritius has seen the establishment besides tourism, of textile and service industries which have transformed the social landscape by creating employment and raising the standard of living of the working class. Mauritius is today quoted as a success story and occupies a respectable place in the league table of developing economies.

Unfortunately, development never comes alone. It brings in its train a series of problems which are the characteristics of a society in the process of industrialisation. Social habits undergo a mutation. While opportunities for young people to share the same factory bench encourage the forging of new friendships, relegating gender and communal consideration into the background, temptations to indulge condemnable habits also winks from the street corner. Weaker characters easily fall prey to them and stray into the dangerous world of gambling and addictive drugs.

I have devoted a story to each of the two deadliest social evils. Gambling and drugs have reached a dimension that is threatening the very stability of family life. Thefts, hold-ups and frauds often related to the two evils are of common occurrence, no longer making front page news. The price of industrialisation is sometimes heavy in terms of social consequences. We have to take it in our stride because we have no other option. We can't have our cake and eat it.

Whatever may be the shortcomings of the stories for which I assume full responsibility, I can give the assurance they have been written with the scrupulous avoidance of any hint to give offence to any individual or group of individuals or their religions or cultural susceptibilities. All the characters in the stories, except those in *The Temple in the Sea*, are fictitious. If by mere coincidence, any person feels any affinity or identity with any of them, I deeply regret it and offer my apologies. I have written the stories with a sincerity of purpose because each of them carries a message which I hope will be understood.

~ The Estate Watchman ~

Rural life in the thirties revolved around the sugar estate, the main employer of labour. Its tied labour force was housed in camps, rows of mud walls supporting a wooden frame covered with cane trash. The labourers were not provided with any recreation. A cultural life of sorts centred around the temple serviced by a priest known as *poosaree.* Once a year, the fire-walking ceremony permitted a break in the monotony and drabness of life in the camps.

There was a time when each estate had its own milling facilities. With the advent of advanced technology, they were found to be uneconomical and they gave way to larger units with a highly mechanized content. The lonely giant chimneys jutting out of the cane fields are the only remaining vestiges of that past. They are now preserved as part of our national heritage.

When the estate became over-populated, a settlement was created adjoining it, which acquired, in the course of time, the status of a village with its shop, school, post office, public fountain and metalled road. The estate which had been the scene of this tragic story, had long lost its factory and its cane was hauled on light tramways to a mill two miles away. Bullock carts transported planters' harvest to the local weighbridge, there to be hand loaded on the tram-wagon. Children took a mischievous pleasure in walking behind the cart to pilfer cane and run away with their prize before the carter's eye could catch them. Sometimes he would raise his whip to scare the delinquents. But it was fun all round.

The crop season was a time of intense activity. The inhabitants seemed happy as there was plenty of work for everybody not only for the labourers. The tailor had a busy time stitching new suits in anticipation of the New Year. The shoemaker, after months of slow activity, suddenly found himself deluged with orders with which he could hardly cope. The shopkeeper had to renew his stock and expected not only to recover his money for the credit sales during the lean inter-crop days, but also to make extra money from increased business. Every Sunday, hawkers stomped the camps and the adjoining village touting their wares. Activities which were suspended between two harvests suddenly seemed to vibrate. Sunday was not only a day of rest, but also an occasion to indulge in intoxicating liquor followed by a few brawls. People congregated at the village shop, the popular meeting place, in their Sunday best.

But the harvest season was also the time of year when poor labourers would make savings for the wedding of their daughters. Any girl above fourteen was already a burden and had to be married to avoid malicious gossip at the village fountain where women met to exchange the latest rumours.

The end of the harvest normally spelt the gloom of hard times. Labourers employed during harvest became redundant, and were laid off. Those who were kept on saw their task increased and were often made to redo the work because of unsatisfactory results. At the end of the month the tied labourers living on estate camps were paid partly in cash and partly in kind, which consisted of poor quality rice and pulses, coconut oil and coarse grained salt. They were rations more fit for animals than humans. The freelance were remunerated on the basis of work done. More often than not, the latter's weekly pay packet hardly amounted to two rupees and a half, out of which, when they had reimbursed the advances from the *sirdar*, very little was left. Without the Chinese shopkeeper to come to the rescue with some credit sales to be reimbursed during harvest, famine would stalk most households.

A few labourers managed to be slightly better off. Their women kept a cow as a source of extra income from the milk, the manure and the calf. Others cultivated a plot in the backyard to supplement the rice menu with some vegetables.

Those who kept a cow or goats, had to collect fodder from the estate as they had no land of their own. During the harvest, the easily available sugar cane tops provided the forage. The problem arose during the inter crop season. The estate sometimes issued permits, against a small fee, to allow the womenfolk to collect fodder in certain areas where plantations would not be interfered with. There was no herbicide in those days and the paths between the cane fields were covered with grass. Those were the days when villagers used as firewood, twigs collected from land under bush. The Condé bush was abundant, growing everywhere where land was allowed to lie fallow. The bush was a valuable source of fuel.

But the access to fodder or fuel was not easy. It depended on the goodwill of the watchmen and especially Major, the head watchman, a hefty six foot giant with a savage mien, striking terror not only among the helpless women out to collect fodder, but also among the men folk, none of whom dared to challenge his insolence and arrogance. He was strong, employed in a job with a potential to do harm, carrying the seal of protection of the estate manager. In other words, he was a powerful person who could get away with any crime. The village women, out of fear, would either avoid him or pay their respect by greeting him with a '*Bonjour Missié*'. He would not even reply, so contemptuous was he of them. It was rumoured that besides the savagery of his behaviour, he had also the reputation of a lecherous disposition. On the estate camp during the sega nights, he would choose any partner for a dance and no one dared to refuse. It was openly said that he had amorous affairs with several women. On Saturday evenings, at the local shop, he would just walk in, and after a few drinks, would storm out when asked to pay. The estate manager was aware of his fracas but observed the silence of an accomplice. Many a time, the brutality of his conduct and the menace he represented for the safety and security of the village women were raised in *baitkhas*[1] but no one was bold enough to suggest any measure to cool his ardour. What was worse, the very next day he would become aware of what was said against him. He would come in the evening to the shop and thunder with threats of mayhem against anyone who had the courage to come face to face to repeat his impertinence. He had the reputation of being a violent man who had done bodily harm to several helpless labourers but no case was ever reported to the police.

In the village there was a young girl who had just married into a family who kept two cows. She had come from a poor but respectable background, brought up according to strict Hindu traditions, handed down over the years and having their origin in the old sacred books. Her marriage was arranged and her upbringing did not permit the questioning of parental decisions. In her new home, a mud hut with two rooms and a small verandah with the cowdung heap in the backyard, she vowed total obedience to her husband and her in-laws. As a bride, she could only find fulfilment in complete integration in her husband's family. Although Rookmeen was leading a drab existence, broken only by an attendance at the fire-walking ceremony where she could display her best dress, and the visit to her parents for the New Year, she showed no signs of unhappiness.

Rookmeen had brought a freshness and a sense of well-being into her conjugal household. Thanks to her kind nature and pleasant manner, she had conquered the heart of her mother-in-law, no mean achievement for a Hindu bride. She was liked by everybody in the village and the mother-in-law was complimented for selecting a girl like Rookmeen as her daughter-in-law.

1. Meeting place of Indian labourers.

Every morning, she used to accompany her mother-in-law and other women to the estate lands to look for fodder. After a few months, she became familiar with the places where grasses were growing abundantly and the mother-in-law had sufficient trust to allow her to operate on her own, within earshot of the other women just to be reassured of their close presence.

Although terrified of the head watchman, the women felt under no threat so long as they were armed with their permit and operated in droves. Major, such was the name of the head watchman, for some time, had noticed the presence of the new girl in full bloom of youth who did not entertain the least apprehension of any risk for her safety. He immediately conceived an evil design but he had to bide his time and wait for the proper opportunity to go for his quarry. So long as the women kept together, he had no chance at all. Any false step would raise the alarm and he would be done for. The moment he was waiting for presented itself one morning almost unexpectedly in a lonely place secluded by tall bushes. The girl, unaware of his presence, was completely absorbed in her task of cutting grasses. He realised an amorous approach would not meet with positive response. He was overtaken by an uncontrollable lust when he saw the young bosom slightly bursting out of the tight blouse. His lechery could not wait. He was aware of the devastating consequences of his act, if caught. But there was nobody and even the girl had not noticed his presence. He was like a wild beast about to fall on his prey and therefore he took precaution to move stealthily before pouncing on her. The girl was so taken by surprise and so afraid by the unexpected assault that she was paralysed and lost her voice. She only made gestures with her hands to implore for mercy and be allowed to go. But he was under the influence of such a beastly desire that nothing could stop him. He lost no time and sexually abused the poor girl, who did not realise what was happening to her. She fell unconscious and the monster abandoned her in that state. It took quite some time before she regained consciousness and became aware of the heinous crime which had reduced her to a heap of filth. She managed to get up and, not to alert any suspicion, avoided the other women on their way home.

She was crushed, reduced to half her strength and lost her usual composure when she reached home. She felt ashamed of her condition, completely lost, not knowing how to confide to her husband who, as Indian husbands normally are, kept aloof from her and had never established that intimacy which made communication easy. As a typical Indian wife, she was in the habit of carrying out orders without the right of complaint. Now she was faced with the most trying time as a young bride. She had a bath to clean herself and prayed at the family shrine. But as it was not a normal practice to bathe at that hour, both her husband and mother-in-law tried to taunt her by querying whether she was observing some special promise made to the family deity. She felt cornered and for the first time since her married life, took her husband aside and confided to him in tears what had taken place. The husband almost had a heart attack. He became cold and was on the point of collapse. After he partially recovered, his first instinct told him to avenge himself by going straight for the aggressor and killing him. But then when he realized that even armed with a weapon he could not measure up to Major, he thought otherwise. The best course would be to report the rape to the police. The mother was consulted; in spite of her outraged feelings, she counselled discretion. A report to the police would give publicity to the whole horrendous incident and neighbours might start talking by giving distorted versions. The watchman had the protection of the estate manager and there was no guarantee that the police would not be biased and turn the table against Rookmeen. She might come out worse and the family's reputation would be so tarnished as to become untenable. Although the husband and the in-laws were horrified, they were helpless. They were too poor to afford a lawyer. They did not want at the same time to antagonise the estate manager, assuming that the latter would side with the watchman. Their livelihood depended upon his goodwill. And worst of all, that monster of a watchman might plead that the girl had consented, having agreed to meet him in a secluded area away from the presence of the other women collecting fodder. The advice of the mother carried the day as it was agreed that it was the soundest course to follow.

But the daughter-in-law, although the victim, did not henceforth enjoy the same consideration. In the eyes of the rest of the family, she had become impure. The husband, Bhajan, cold-shouldered her and the mother-in-law began to make all sorts of insinuations, most hurtful to her self-respect. It was even suggested that she might have concocted the rape story to conceal an adulterous act. Neighbours suspected, in the treatment meted out to her, some serious misbehaviour on her part. From a victim of a heinous crime, Rookmeen was gradually being turned into a culprit. Her life was becoming unbearable. At the public fountain where women used to congregate more for a gossip than a bucket of water, comments were freely traded and it was being said that the girl had fallen into disgrace for serious misconduct. The days were not far off when she would be sent back to her parents. In the meantime, she was ostracized by the family, not being given any work to do. She had ceased accompanying her mother-in-law, or going on her own, with other women, to fetch fodder.

Meanwhile, Major was behaving as if nothing had happened. But he was feeling uneasy and waited for reactions. He felt reassured when a week passed without any suspicion being aroused. For him the matter had been closed. The girl might not have said anything to anyone. Out of shame she might have kept the whole matter to herself. He felt confident that no report had been made to the Police because no inquiry had started. He continued his visit to the village shop with the same arrogance as before. But he was anxious. He thought that if, sooner or later, information that he had raped the girl would leak out, he would not be left at peace for long. He avoided the women out to collect fodder because their antagonistic attitude made him feel a suspect but he was still powerful and no one had the courage to lift an accusing finger at him.

A month passed and the fate of the girl became worse. She was made to feel unwanted. Not a day passed without her being subjected to humiliating insinuations. She thought of committing suicide, but postponed the fatal decision hoping that her last resort, a refuge at her parents' place might grant her a reprieve.

One day, much to the relief of her husband and her in-laws, she left for her mother's place, a village away. Her predicament was known to her parents, but at the same time the malicious rumour concerning her disgrace had also spread among close members of her family and neighbours. The mother welcomed her daughter and was shattered by her tale of woe. The brother, who had already been given some version of her misfortune, wanted to know the truth. He was troubled in his mind that his sister could lose her virtue without anyone, especially her husband, trying to find redress. After much hesitation, she related to him in detail what had taken place and the reaction of her husband and her in-laws, and the viciousness with which she was treated and even turned into a culprit by malicious innuendoes. She found no sympathy anywhere. She had come back to her parents hoping to find solace but Indian society is one of the most cruel; instead of giving the moral support she badly needed, she was considered a burden. A Hindu girl once married has to accept her fate for good or bad. She belongs to her husband and, if rejected by him even without any justification, she will find no place in society. Her parents have no moral duty to receive her and give her hospitality. However upright her conduct, she is always presumed to be wrong and is given no opportunity to plead her innocence.

The mother felt strongly for her daughter but the fact that she was sent away by her husband put her in an awkward position. There was a rumour, rightly or wrongly, being circulated regarding her ejection from the conjugal roof. Besides there was another young daughter of marriageable age, who might not find a match if the elder one stayed around. She did not say anything to hurt her daughter at the beginning, but when neighbours started gossiping, she told Rookmeen to return to her husband regardless of the fate reserved for her. After a few weeks she could not face the neighbours who turned their back and avoided her. She could not work as none was available. Some women even went to the length of suggesting she could be a bad influence on young unmarried girls. Driven to the extreme, with her back to the wall, she had only one course open to her: to commit suicide. She realised that neither her parents nor her husband and his family could fight against the dark forces which preyed upon a backward society, like the one in which she was born and brought up. She accepted the reality of the situation and one evening left the house and threw herself into a well, favoured, because of its depth, by suicide candidates. Her absence raised the alarm. The brother knew that she had gone to her death. The mother's instinct led to the same conclusion. Two days later after some search, the body was recovered and Rookmeen was cremated on her father's sugar cane land.

She was mourned by all the neighbours. Even the husband and the in-laws turned up with a guilty conscience. They had all conspired to bring about her death and now were shedding tears, even proclaiming that she was a good innocent girl. But in their heart, her death was a good riddance. She would soon be forgotten and life would resume its normal course and no one would even try to analyse the rottenness of the society which led to her suicide.

The brother, Bhim, however, became moody. He was a man of

some education having moved in the society of people who were questioning the causes which were keeping them in wretched conditions. They were trying to understand why they were the weaker segment of the multiracial community, having made a virtue of their cringing acceptance of dominance and humiliation. They had become too inert as a race to react against the moral and mental bondage.

The crime of which his sister was a victim was turned against her owing to the cowardice of his people and the abject fear of standing up against it; the most despicable example was her husband. Should he in turn sink to the same level of distasteful conduct by refusing to avenge the honour of a sister because of the risks involved? If he were not to act, who would? He deliberated on the duty of a brother, he reminded himself of the heroes in the Scriptures to whom he turned, in moments of crisis, for inspiration. He did not believe in the justice of his country because it was always loaded against the weak, especially the Indians. It was a wise decision not to report to the police. His sister could have come out sullied as a person who might have consented. He struggled within himself for two nights after the cremation, and racked his brain to finally reach the irrevocable decision to avenge his sister by taking the law in his hands, with the full knowledge that the price would be heavy, may even cost him his life. He was not a man to recoil before any obstacle once his mind was made up.

He laid out a plan with a precision that left nothing to chance. First he had to know the movement of his intended quarry, the watchman. Secondly he had to make sure of overpowering him with a first blow and then to kill him. Face to face he was no match and he was bound to lose. It had to be a surprise attack with a lethal weapon. He therefore decided on an ambush. In anticipation of his attack, he began to follow Major's round on the estate very secretly, especially at the time when he used to wander off to remote parts away from any human presence. He made sure that his habit followed a pattern to which he was strictly faithful.

The news of the suicide of Rookmeen spread like wildfire. Comments were made in profusion by people who knew her. Most were now sympathetic and held her husband and his parents responsible. Others accused society for its cruelty and prejudices to victims of such aggressions. Those who were most sympathetic were the non-Hindus, especially the Christians, to whom charity had a resonance in every case of injustice and victimisation. Although there was strong suspicion about the identity of her aggressor few dared make an open accusation.

The watchman to whom the news of Rookmeen's suicide came as a rude shock was really shaken. For the first time, he was afraid. He felt death stalking him and he was quite uneasy. He tried to put a brave front and continued with his normal habits. But the bravado had left him. He was less arrogant although he faced the public and took his drinks without paying. He suffered from sleeplessness and was losing his appetite. His wife noticed the change but dared not ask the reason. He even thought of emigrating from the village but gave it up as a sign of defeatism and a confirmation of suspicion.

However cowardly a person may be, if pushed to the brink, he may turn violent, and then even those physically superior in strength have to be careful. Who knows what was going in the mind of the husband, Bhajan, who was no doubt aware of the whole abomination? Major was racked by such thoughts and was afraid. Two weeks had passed and Bhim, the brother, relentlessly watched for an opportunity. He knew by now where to ambush him and at what time. The place chosen was in the thick of the sugar plantation. The canes at that time of the year had grown tall and were so dense that the roads between the fields looked dark and sinister. It was the time when Major used to make his last round just in case he might fall upon some rare rugged villagers collecting fodder or firewood in the estate woodlands, a prohibited area reserved for deer hunting by the manager. Twice Bhim waited and, on both occasions, he refrained from acting because he wanted to study Major's slightest behaviour and movement and he also wanted to make sure that the place he had chosen to hide himself was secure and his presence would not be detected. It was the third time that he found the occasion favourable for his design. When the watchman had covered a certain distance, he came out very gingerly out of his hiding and armed with a heavy stick walked steadily behind him and dealt him such a blow on the head that Major fell instantly unconscious without having time to utter a sound. Bhim fell upon him and plunged a dagger in his chest. To be satisfied that he had finished him, he slit his throat. Having completed his task he dragged the body inside the field and covered it with trash. He then walked towards a stream, washed his hand of blood, and threw away the dagger. He felt a peace descending upon him. Now that he had avenged his sister and given the punishment that was due to the perpetrator of the monstrous crime, he went back home. He knew that sooner or later, the police would knock at his door. Suspicion would inevitably fall upon him, not upon his brother-in-law, Bhajan, who was too much of a wimp, a shameful coward.

Major's wife, who was accustomed to his frequent nocturnal escapades, did not raise the alarm when he did not return home for the night. His absence was also noticed at the shop. When he did not report for duty in the morning speculation began to circulate; one theory was that he had eloped with a woman, another theory was that he had taken leave and gone to spend the day with a relative in another village. It was on the third day after his death that a real search began, when it was feared that he had met his destiny in the hands of his match to whom he might have done serious harm. It was not difficult to find the body in the initial stages of decomposition. Part of the flesh was missing, some predators like the mongoose must have torn some pieces off.

His death was received almost with jubilation. Not a single individual in the village, irrespective of race or religion, showed any commiseration. The unanimous verdict was that his violent death was a just retribution for all his misdeeds. It was even openly stated that he was the aggressor who had raped the girl and driven her to her death.

The post mortem had revealed the extent of the mutilation done to his body. It was as if the person who had killed had undertaken to torture him and hack his body in a spirit of blind revenge. Great publicity was given to the assassination. Some newspapers were satisfied with the version of the estate manager who gave as motive, the elimination of a faithful servant performing his duty with all the severity that his responsibility demanded. At his funeral, paid for by the estate, only a handful of people were present, besides members of his family. Even his two assistants did not express any regret. They were at one with the majority of the inhabitants.

As he died on duty, the estate manager summoned the district top brass of the police and enjoined upon them an immediate inquiry and quick results. In other words, even torture had to be used to get the culprit.

The inquiry was entrusted to an Inspector well-known for his obsequiousness to the rich and powerful. In this particular case, he went all out to produce quick results to ingratiate himself with the estate manager. His method fitted the stereotype and he used informers recruited in the village. A five-rupee note, in those days, could take him a long way towards putting him on the right track. He learnt that there was a suspicion that the victim had sexually assaulted and raped Rookmeen, wife of Bhajan. His first suspect was inevitably Bhajan, the husband, who was arrested and put in custody in a police cell. His arrest caused a small commotion as nobody could believe he was capable of the smallest violence, coward and ineffectual as he was. But one never knows!

Fortunately for him besides clamouring his innocence, he gave useful information to the police which, as a next step, led them to inquire into the circumstances of the suicide. Who could be the culprit, except somebody closely related to the girl and desperately intent upon revenge? The inevitable conclusion was the brother as the next suspect. In the meantime, the husband was still kept in custody. In those days, there was no question of obtaining legal assistance. Barristers were a species unknown to people of his condition; struggling to keep alive below the poverty line, how could he pay for the services of a lawyer?

The police were relentlessly pursuing their inquiry and the net was now closing in on Bhim. Information had reached the Inspector that he was seen in the vicinity of the Major's beat a few days before the murder. There was no doubt that he was the man. He had all the motives to undertake such a gruesome mission. It was his sister who, from her ashes, was crying for revenge. Bhim was not surprised when he heard the heavy boots of a posse of police at his doorstep. He did not offer any resistance. Handcuffed, he was taken in a van to the nearest station where he saw his brother-in-law. His mother and sister were beating their breasts, as if the son was not going to be seen again. They could not understand why Bhim had been arrested. He was such a good boy. Why on earth should misfortune dog them in such succession? After the loss of Rookmeen, now the apple of the mother's eyes, the only son, being taken away from them. Neighbours had gathered, each with a comment. The scene was heart-breaking. But everybody was helpless. Fate had to take its toll.

Bhim had decided to make a clean breast to the police. It was a decision taken even before his arrest. He had committed the crime and as a man he had to face up to it. That would exonerate his brother-in-law. His confession was a triumph to the Inspector in charge of the inquiry. He had got the culprit. He knew he would be rewarded with a promotion. The estate manager would throw all his weight to persuade the Superintendent to give due recognition to his diligence and efficiency.

Bhim was charged with murder and after an appearance before the District Magistrate, was remanded to Beau Bassin prison. His brother-in-law was released, as it was evident he was innocent. Bhim was to stay in remand for almost a year before he was tried at the Assizes. In the meantime, his relatives and friends met in a Defence Committee to raise money to pay the lawyer. The press had hailed the Inspector as an outstanding detective. But what surprised most people was the daring act of Bhim, an Indian labourer, who had the temerity and courage to kill an estate watchman, a six footer, vested with vast authority. If the Indian had gone that far, then the estate authority must watch out. He had set a bad example and those docile Indians should no longer be trusted. Behind their meekness and wimpishness they were concealing great potential for causing damage. Bhim must be given a punishment to deter others from similar acts.

The defence committee had, after much solicitation, succeeded in raising a sum of Rs 500. The services were retained of a barrister, a coloured man known for his sense of justice and his outspokenness against an oligarchy which had taken over the control of all the key posts in the judiciary and the Parquet, not to mention the Police. He warned he had an uphill task because he had to fight not only for justice, but against a system which was so rotten that justice had long lost its true meaning. Nonetheless he accepted the brief.

When he learnt of the confession, he became helpless. How could he defend Bhim when the confession had closed all loopholes and all the elements for a cast-iron murder case were present – the intention to kill, the premeditation, the malice aforethought, and the death? He tried to find out whether the confession was voluntary or extorted. Bhim maintained it was voluntary. Again the counsel reminded him that when the murder took place there was no witness, so why did he confess? When the lawyer was convinced that Bhim was holding his ground, he told him to expect the worse. He told the relatives that the son had confessed and there was no defence against murder. He could only try to appeal to the Governor on grounds of mercy to have the death sentence, which was mandatory in murder cases, commuted to life imprisonment.

On learning of the possible consequences, the mother fell unconscious and was ill for several days. Friends and neighbours comforted her and counselled her to undertake a period of penance by fasting once or twice a week and praying to *Shivji*[2]. She did not mind the imprisonment, it was the death sentence that had wrecked her mentally and physically.

We were in the year 1935. King George V who had been on the throne for twenty-five years had fixed his Silver Jubilee Celebration in July. Preparations were in full swing. School children were rehearsing 'Britannia rules the waves' and 'God Save the King'. They were told about a king whom they never expected to see, but they were all proud to belong to the Empire, a concept no one bothered to define. In all the towns there were decorations and illuminations. Port Louis, as the capital, had organised special events to mark the great occasion. All the main streets were decorated. At night there were illuminations and fireworks and the Chinese traders had organised a dragon procession. During the day, a race meeting with Jubilee Cup was the highlight of the celebrations. The whole country was in a festive mood. Trainloads of people travelled to Port Louis for the races and the illumination. For once the population had forgotten its daily anguish and deprivation and in a big surge of jubilation

2. The Hindu God.

had joined to express its contentment as a far-flung corner of the Empire, the existence of which was hardly known in the corridors of Whitehall.

But in the middle of all the joys and cheerfulness there was one family sunk in gloom and desperation. Bhim, as was foreseen, had been sentenced to death a month before. His lawyer had petitioned for mercy taking advantage of an amnesty declared in favour of certain prisoners to give the jubilee an additional significance. The Governor had ordered a stay of execution by not fixing the date. As it was the only case awaiting execution of the death sentence, he wanted to study the file before accepting to sully his hands with the blood of a human being in the twenty-fifth year of grace of the reign of His Majesty George V. To the indignation and surprise of the establishment, he commuted the death sentence into one of life imprisonment, which meant 15 years out of which Bhim could get a remission of five years for good conduct. The news was greeted with much relief and joy by the relatives and friends of Bhim. The counsel who had finally triumphed by saving him from the gallows was welcomed as a hero and garlanded in a reception in his honour. What influenced the Governor to reverse the death sentence was the strong plea made by the Counsel in the petition, which had underlined the stress under which the brother had acted, the unpunished crime of rape which led to the suicide of the girl, the terror in which the whole village was living as a result of the brutality of the watchman who derived his authority from the estate manager. He had further laid emphasis on the state of the society which had its own code of morality, a code which encouraged hushing up cases of rape to save the family from disgrace and public censor. The happiest person was the mother who attributed to God and her penance, the survival of her son. Ten years were preferable to the terrible agony of death. She became religious and prayed everyday for the safe return of Bhim.

Ten years were a long time to those who had to wait. Her daughter had married and she was a grandmother. Her husband had died. She did not care to inquire about Bhajan, her ex-son-in-law and his family. World War II came and changed the life of the country. Several thousands had joined the army and were away for a few years. In 1945, when Bhim finally returned home he found himself in a world which had undergone fundamental changes. The new generation which returned from the army refused to accept the *status quo*. Workers were organised and had learned to strike. The arrogance of the estate manager and brutality of his watchmen belonged to the past. The young Indians who had joined the army had shed most of their timidity and inhibitions. There was talk of constitutional conferences and the right of vote. Bhim gradually adapted to these new surroundings in which he discovered dignity and happiness. He decided to devote the rest of his life to combating the injustice of Hindu Society which was still immersed in superstitions and obsolete beliefs, all designed to keep members in darkness. He remained a celibate and by his exemplary conduct inspired many young people to stand up for the dignity and welfare of the women folk. He died a monument of courage and fearlessness.

~ The Sound of the Drum ~

Introductory Notes

The story that follows takes place in the year 1930 and the scene is set in a predominantly Indian village, an overspill from the local sugar estate camps. All the characters are fictitious and even the wedding ceremony is pure invention although it gives a faithful description of the celebrations which, through the years, have changed considerably in their particulars, although not in substance, by shedding all the unsocial aspects and demeaning features. Hindu society is still plagued with the curse of the caste system although on a much smaller scale than in the thirties. Its practice is fast fading. The community has long been set on the path of a levelling process by inter caste matrimonial alliances.

It is without contest that we have travelled a long way from the dark days of the thirties. But the struggle is not over – it must go on until the last vestige of social discrimination is eradicated.

The drama of the Head Teacher in the story is a reminder of the vulnerability of our social system. That reminder should be an eye opener because we are now faced with another menace from the new found evangelists who are working havoc among our youth with their promise of a new Jerusalem. I may be accused of jingoism for raising an issue confined to a section when the general talk is about national unity. On serious reflection it will be agreed that the path to national unity should not be scattered with fragmented communities. In addition, I have also a duty to record, for the benefit of our children, those murky chapters of our history, without a knowledge of which the present holds no meaning. The tendency to obliterate the saga of our humiliations and shortcomings should be resisted by all those who care for a true version of our past. The modicum of dignity and justice which we all enjoy today has been the outcome of a struggle soaked with tears and blood, fought both within and without the community.

The message of the story is loud and clear for everybody. Let it not be lost in a maze of controversial interpretations.

Sir Satcam Boolell, QC

~ The Sound of the Drum ~

Dalit Mahajan had fixed the wedding of his daughter, after consultation with the Pandit and the groom's family, for December 21st 1930. The Pandit had not chosen the date arbitrarily, he was guided by the stars. The date had to be propitious otherwise the marriage would not bring happiness and prosperity. That December could be very hot, over 32°C, with cyclone and heavy rains in gestation in the Mozambique Canal and threatening to visit the island without much of a warning, was of no consequence. The stars had spoken and nature would have to suspend its mischief. Such was, and still is, the strong belief of the Hindus in the Brahmin priest, the only one habilitated to interpret the scriptures and no other force could intervene to shake that belief.

The preparation for the big occasion began. List of guests had to be prepared. We were already in August and the invitation had to be sent at least a month in advance. In the meantime visits between the families of the bride and the groom began to be multiplied. Already the news of the projected marriage had spread in the village. Mahajan was a rich planter and the Wedding Ceremony was to be the event of the year. Mahajan was a man of reputation known for his strong views on Hindu religious practices. He was President of the local temple and his orthodoxy brooked no relaxation of the strict adherence to tradition. He was usually clad in a white dhoti reaching to his ankles, a mark of distinction denoting a good caste. He had the biggest house, almost a mansion, with a verandah and a long drive. Every afternoon he used to hold court in his verandah and receive his visitors. Tea would be served to those belonging to the proper castes. The lower orders would only approach him in moments of need, for example a loan, and the interview would not last long. Exceptions were made for the few who had property or influence. Police officers were frequent visitors and they were well entertained and always loaded with gifts durıng the New Year. Mahajan often organised gandia session after the weekly Ramayan recital. Most of the villagers were poor and they had a high respect for him, the more so because of his relationship with the Police. It was a time when the sugar price had reached its lowest level and many planters had seen their land foreclosed because of their inability to pay their debt. Mahajan was also a money lender and in the best tradition of Indian money lenders charged high rates of interest. Those who could not refund him lost their land and every so often Mahajan increased his freehold.

Labour was cheap and there were no labour laws to fix the wages, trade Unions were unheard of. Labourers were at the mercy of the planters who could squeeze their last drop of blood and starve them. The workers survived by the expedient of keeping a cow and selling its milk and cultivating some vegetables in their backyard. Although life was simple the workers were engaged from dawn till dusk in the struggle for survival.

Mahajan's daughter was called Lutchmeen, the young man to whom she was engaged to be married bore the name of Pahlad. Lutchmeen had never been to school and therefore had no knowledge of French or English, but she knew a little Hindi and could recite the Ramayan. She had also been taught, in view of her marriage, some household work such as cooking, and stitching patterns on canvas for bed covers and pillow cases. She had also learnt ironing just in case. She was very attractive, having inherited the fair complexion of her mother and the fine features of her father. At eighteen she was in the full bloom of youth, exuding vitality and a purity of heart expressed in her gentleness and kindness. She had never met Pahlad and did not know how he looked but her parents could be trusted to make the right choice. Pahlad was the eldest son of Mahasay, of the same caste, two villages away, but not as rich as Dalit. He was known as Lalit Mahasay. Pahlad, a young man of twenty-four, with a deportment proclaiming his good breeding and the allure of an intellectual, after years of perseverance had qualified as a teacher, having passed his examinations most successfully, Fourth, Third and Second Class. He was offered a job in the village Catholic school, in a junior capacity. In a few years he was promoted to the rank of third class teacher. The Roman Catholic authorities appreciated his work, but the Head Teacher retained a certain reservation: he thought that the young man was too pretentious and too much of a braggart. Pahlad spoke good French and knew his grammar well, having mastered Claude Augé. Although not as proficient in English he had sufficient mastery to command respect of his colleagues. As a teacher he was popular with the pupils, and his score at the examination of Standard VI was among the best in his area. He was refusing private tuition, preferring to give more time to his class. The Area Inspector was full of praise and gave him good marks, to be used advantageously in assessing him for promotion, but the Roman Catholic authorities had other pre-occupations – Pahlad was a Hindu and a staunch one at that. Priority for promotion normally went to Catholic staff, irrespective of merit or seniority. The possibility of bringing him into the Catholic fold could not be envisaged. He would rather sacrifice his job rather than his religion. The Head Teacher resented the proud profession of his faith and the observance of all his religious festivals, although not a single one was, at that time recognised as entitling him to special leave.

But Pahlad did not mind being sidelined for promotion. He knew he belonged to a religious denominational school, not his own, and he could not expect to be given the treatment of government servants. Those were the days when only strong characters could hold their ground and resist pressure of proselytisation. The weaker characters who were more vulnerable accepted to change their faith, abjure their relations and community for a post and for better security. Conversion to Christianity meant more than a belief in a new religious faith. It meant total repudiation of one's culture, tradition, name and family. It was like a crossing of the Rubicon by severing all links with one's past. It meant also being ashamed of that past and an avoidance of all reference to it. It meant a reincarnation into a new life, with consummate amnesia. Such was the strong pull, that the newly converted became strangers to their own people, looking down upon them and even harbouring a hatred for them.

Their attempt, however, to join the mainstream of the coloured section with comparable intellectual level, was spurned because their pedigree was considered inferior to that of the upper layers of Rose Hill and Beau Bassin. The absence of affinity with the Afro-creoles, except a common religious belief, was a strong inhibiting factor making social intercourse with the latter scarce and far between. The desire to avoid the risk of stagnating in a limbo drove them to join together with their own kind and thus constitute a separate community. In the course of time they developed into a powerful intellectual group with a strong hold in the administration and the liberal professions. They produced brilliant lawyers, physicians and administrative cadres. Although close to Western culture the majority nonetheless kept their patronymic identity, as a link to their ancestral root.

Pahlad had no such inhibition. His Society provided him with the freedom to develop his faculties and live a life of fulfilment and satisfaction. He had no problem of social mobility. He was accepted in every milieu in his community. In short he was more than satisfied with his station and entertained no ambition to imitate his neighbours over the fence. His modest salary was more than adequate to meet his needs. He could even save, not only for a rainy day but also to add to his sugar lands. To get married and create a family posed no problem. In his extended family system his wife would be a welcome addition as an extra hand in the kitchen and a help in other domestic chores. The house was large enough to spare an extra room for his bride and himself. Food was cooked and shared in common.

The day of the wedding was fast approaching. We were already in November. All the preparations were well under way, invitations had been sent, the services of the officiating priest and the family barber had been retained. Pahlad would now and then pay a visit to his future in-laws to be posted about how preparations were progressing. His future father-in-law was proud of the match and would brag to his friends about the intellectual accomplishment of his future son in law. He would mention Pahlad's conversation with the Police Inspector in French and how the latter was easy game to him. He also used to remind the gullible villagers of the day when Pahlad had accompanied him to Port Louis to meet the Deputy of the District, a distinguished barrister of white extraction, and how he was proud to see him conversing in both French and English. Pahlad was aware of his future father-in-law's infatuation and felt inwardly flattered. The question of musicians and singers was one day discussed. Dalit wanted the wedding an event to be remembered. He insisted on the Police Band, whatever the cost, but as a good orthodox Hindu the drum for the *Do Mela*[1] was a must. It was an important part of the ceremony to have music when the groom's party reached the bride's place and formed a procession to be greeted by their counterparts, when the two prospective fathers-in-law gave themselves the traditional accolade with water and silver coins. It was moving to see the musicians, just before the meeting of the two groups, positioning themselves

1. Meeting of the bride's and bridegroom's guests before the wedding ceremony.

in the middle to herald the accolade by first striking a note on a low key to gradually build up into a crescendo in a spirit of contest. It was a music highly symbolic of the great event to take place. The emotion it unleashed could only be appreciated by those who knew the importance of the role of that group of musicians without whose contribution the wedding ceremony would be incomplete because it would be robbed of one of its most religious contents. The music not only enhanced the ceremony but introduced a solemnity and a spiritual presence. It reached its highest pitch when after the accolade the two groups joined together to symbolise the merging of two families into one.

According to age old tradition those who played the drum had to acquire special skills and normally belonged to a particular social order. Their role, after the meeting of the two groups, came to an end and they were consigned to a corner, away from the main ceremony. From then on their services would not be required until the next day. In the village the man who used to be the drummer at the weddings was known as Dhania.

He was very poor, with three children, all of a tender age. Life was hard for people like Dhania. He was a labourer and earned hardly enough to feed his family. Fortunately he had his own hut and so had a refuge from the toils of the day. The wedding ceremony was a windfall as he could earn a rupee or two depending on the hirer. As a labourer he was earning 40 cs for a whole day's work. Although rice was at 5 cs a pound he could not give enough to his children to eat. His wife also worked on and off to supplement their meagre earnings.

Those were the days when, except for the rich, everybody went barefoot. Their bed consisted of a straw mattress on a wooden frame and the cover was made of hessian sheets. There were no chairs or table. The feeble light was provided by a petrol lamp, a fire hazard, made of tin with an old piece of cloth as a wick. The interior of the hut was dark with no window for light or ventilation. Hygiene was totally absent. All the tropical diseases like malaria, dysentery, pneumonia, ankylosis, etc were rife. Medical care was not available. People used to have recourse to herbal medicine and witchcraft in case of illness. Their life span was not even thirty years of age.

Indian labourers, worn out at an early age by hard work in the sugar cane fields, were undernourished and most vulnerable to disease. They were physically weak, with early loss of teeth and with greying hair. They were perforce meek, gentle and always subservient and the target of all others who were physically better nourished. The poor Indian constantly lived in fear and, in the face of the worst humiliation, offered no opposition. The Indian labourer was the most pathetic figure in the village. His only break from the monotony of his abject condition was the religious festival, like Holi, and the weddings to which, although not invited, he would still go near enough to listen to the folk music and the songs. A curse followed him from birth through to his death. He lived without hope. He hung on to life because he was afraid to die.

Although December was a hot month, nights were pleasant. But December was unfortunately also the time of the year when tropical rain could just pour to the accompaniment of thunder and lightning. That wedding night rain did fall and Dhania with only the mango tree to shelter him was wet through. But he dared not leave, because Mahajan had not rewarded him and he was still waiting to be fed. When practically all the wedding guests had eaten and departed somebody noticed the presence of Dhania and his fellow musicians and on learning that they had not been served, some food was doled out, cold chappattis and dhal. Dhania's appetite had long abandoned him. He was shivering and coughing. He was feverish. He did not touch the food and preferred to retire to his house not far away. In bed he was still shivering and a double hessian sheet did not provide any warmth.

He had a high temperature yet he was obsessed by the feeling that he might not be able to find a replacement for the last part of the wedding ceremony the following morning. He was afraid his absence might result in the forfeiture of his reward. Besides he did not want and could not afford to cause any inconvenience or indisposition to the Mahajan. So he came back in the morning for the last rite although with a high temperature.

In the meantime the Mahajan and his family were too busy receiving the newly married couple and looking after the close relatives who had to partake of the post wedding lunch to have a thought for Dhania and company. The latter went back home without seeing Mahajan. In other words the meagre reward on which he had counted so much was not forthcoming. Dhania fell seriously ill. The local shaman was helpless, neighbours were generous in advice, but no one could make a loan to call a doctor. The hospital was too far away and therefore was out of question. An ambulance service did not exist. Two days later Dhania was in a coma and the third day he died. Mahajan was too important to pay a call. He sent news he would send a cartload of wood for the cremation. The local Brahmin performed a quick service and left with a small fee. Friends and neighbours had contributed for the cremation and the religious rites. Mahajan had given the wood and considered himself relieved of the small recompense he owed for the wedding music.

Dhania had left a widow and three small children, for her the future was bleak. Some charitable souls gave some aid to tide them over for a few days. But that was all. Mrs Dhania, who was a brave and practical woman, girded herself to face the future and decided to join the female gang of labourers on the sugar estate. After a few weeks she began to complete her task and thus earned enough to keep her children from starvation.

Dhania's fate is probably one of thousands whose offspring managed to survive and may be still living without any bitterness for a system which destroyed them and which they took for granted. The tragedy of Dhania does not stem from his social condition only. Others, irrespective of caste, had gone through the same or worse misfortune because the political administration was such as to be absolved of all responsibility for such social calamity.

In the meantime, as readers must have by now realised the wedding and the aftermath were over. It is important to remind ourselves that Pahlad had invited the Head Teacher and staff of his school for the wedding dinner.

Pahlad and his new bride had settled nicely in the extended family. He was a happy man with a wife who could cook, a mother who had adopted her as her daughter and in laws who held him in high esteem. He was aware of the prospect of a good heritage in the future. He had not asked for special leave for his wedding as it coincided with the December holidays.

The Post Wedding

When Pahlad went to school after classes began again in January, he was congratulated by members of the staff, all of whom praised him on his wedding dress and were full of appreciation for the special arrangements to receive them. They had all been invited for the wedding dinner with a special request to the Head Teacher. As all of them were Christians, Pahlad had given instructions to serve them food in a special room. Of course, the Head Teacher, Pierre Watson, was given special attention, but the latter had reserved his judgment and was in a depressed mood. When Pahlad went to see him the reception was cold. Pahlad could not understand the cold shouldering which had been going on for some years but he accepted the treatment even this time with some stoicism. A month later he applied for a day's leave, a rare occurrence in his case, to accompany his wife to a temple in the South, to keep tryst with a promise both had made at the first sign of her pregnancy. The leave was to coincide with the Hindu festival of Shiva Ratri. The Head Teacher categorically refused on the grounds that the school was short of staff. It was the last straw and Pahlad decided the critical moment had arrived when he must find out the reason for such inimical attitude. Pahlad had nothing to reproach himself. His attendance was so regular that the Area Inspector held him out as an example.

He therefore made a bold move one morning to confront him and asked the reason why he had singled him out for his unfair behaviour. Was it because he was a Hindu and therefore a non-Christian? He could not be held responsible for his birth. He was proud of everything he was.

The Head Teacher was not to be provoked. But he was also looking for an opportunity for some time to come out clean with a rancour that was eating him up. At first he shouted in an aggressive tone to remind him of his inferior status in the hierarchy and therefore his impudence to question his authority.

'Who are you to query my decision? You can easily afford to take your wife to your temple on a Saturday or Sunday. As to the auspiciousness of the religious day this is mere superstition in which you Hindus are steeped and which explains your backwardness.'

This time it was Pahlad who felt insulted. 'Mr Watson, I have respect for you as a Head Teacher. Whether you give me leave or not is immaterial. But I will not accept that you insult my religion. I am going to take up the matter with the district member of the Legislative Council, who knows my father-in-law well. I also know him, having visited him with my father in law. Although a non-Christian I have the same right as others because the school is run with tax payers' money.'

The Head Teacher was taken aback. For the first time, he had been confronted with such language from one of his staff, a non-Catholic to boot. The mention of the Honourable member of the

Legislative Council, a white man and a Barrister at law, was enough to make him wince. He was speechless. He realised that Pahlad could mobilize political power to influence the Catholic Authority. Pahlad had stormed out of his office after uttering his threat.

The Head Teacher called him back and all of a sudden became conciliatory. He began by advising Pahlad that he was young, he had a career in front of him and that he should not lose his temper, that he himself was misunderstood, he was not antagonistic to him, because he came from the same stock. Then he related the following story:

'I was a very small boy, hardly five when a man died in circumstances similar to those of Dhania. I was too young to understand that he died of pneumonia contracted on a cold night spent in the open. He also was of the caste which played the drum in the wedding. Instead of being rewarded for his performance he was sent in a remote corner and told to wait to be fed after all the wedding guests had eaten. By the early hours, seeing that no notice was taken of him he went back to his house. The cold he had caught developed into pneumonia and he died through lack of medical care. After his cremation his widow found herself with three small children without any resources. She had never worked in the field and domestic work was not available as it was not in the culture of the villagers to allow strangers to do the washing or cleaning. Besides, they were too poor to give her any help. After struggling for a week or so she was advised to visit the local nuns to offer her services for any job as a domestic. The nuns had heard of her plight and immediately took pity and offered to help. They gave her some money to buy food for her starving children and next day visited her. Seeing the conditions in which she was living they offered her not only a job to wash the linen but also to provide shelter for the children and look after their education. In her desperate situation there was no room for hesitation. The neighbours had failed, she must not spurn the helping hand that was extended to her. Two days later she went to the chief nun with her children and ever since has never looked back. The three boys were baptized and given all the attention needed to make them happy. The mother was given work, accommodation and a small wage. With her children close to her, with no problem for board and lodging she felt relieved and was happy.

'The boys were sent to school and given private tuition for post primary education. The eldest one qualified as a Teacher, was employed by the Catholic Authority and later promoted to be a Head Teacher. The second brother became a Police Sergeant and the third one emigrated to Loreazo Marquez, now Maputo, capital of Mozambique, where he was employed in the railways. The person who is talking to you is the Head Teacher. I am the offspring of that poor Indian who had died in inhumane circumstances because of the ingrained prejudice against a section to which my poor father belonged. My mother had no one to look up to. We would have starved had it not been for those nuns, our benefactresses, of revered memory. Whenever I think of my background and remember my story I feel bitter and wish I could destroy with my curse those who still believe in a system which treats human beings worse than pariah dogs.

'I have nothing against you as an individual, but against the society which by your conduct you want to perpetuate. When I grew up and learnt about the fate of my father I decided to cut off all connections with his community. To make a total commitment of my abhorrence and abjuration I adopted a surname which in the course of years would completely take leave of my roots. I do not want my children to remember their origin. I want to obliterate all memory of my past so that when my children grow up they will have a completely free mind and be able to live the life of their choice. I want to emigrate to a land where nothing is known or heard about this abomination of caste. I know the Catholic religion also is not above considerations of class and colour, but at least there is a possibility of social mobility if not for me, at least for my children, if they acquire the necessary skills and knowledge. I do not pretend that I am happy as I am but at least I have the satisfaction of getting the respect of people like you, which otherwise I would not get had I stayed in the Hindu community, even after attaining the position of a Head Teacher. You and your people would not have given me the treatment you did by making special arrangements to receive me and the other Christian staff. As a Hindu I would have remained an inferior being carrying the stigma of my birth. But as a Christian I am more than your equal. I am your superior and you treat me as such because the role is reversed and you feel inferior in your turn. You may take your leave and let us part without any ill feeling.'

Pahlad was stunned. He was unable to express a word. He remained almost paralysed for a minute and he staggered out of the office, his mind full of thought. He was a transformed man, his eyes were opened. He went back home and told his wife the story of the Head Teacher. She could not believe her ears. She was shocked at the injustice suffered by his father and mother. Immediately their thoughts went to the widow of Dhania and her children. They felt guilty of a heinous crime and for a moment they turned their wrath towards the father, Dalit Mahajan, for his callousness and inhumanity. But of what avail would it be to reprove his behaviour when he was only acting as the product of a system which was corroded, self-destructing and a shame to the human race?

As sensible people, Pahlad and his wife Lutchmeen decided to do the practical things to prove their willingness to make amends by taking under their protection Dhania's widow and her children. She was given employment in the household as a helper to wash the linen, the dishes and even help in the kitchen. Gradually she was made to feel as part of the household. Pahlad's mother, who was at first a little resentful, soon came to terms with her presence when she discovered her cleanliness, her good manners and her ability to prepare tasty dishes.

Dhania's widow was a great blessing to the Pahlad couple. Within a few weeks she changed the aspect of the house, made it look more orderly and clean. The garbage was not swept into a corner but was disposed of far from the kitchen carried in a basket. Pahlad took care of the children's education, bearing always in mind the example of the Head Teacher.

The news of the benevolence of Pahlad and his wife spread in the village and while most people approved of it, others were sceptical, holding the view that he would soon get over his newly acquired altruistic reforming zeal and lapse into the old rut. Pahlad let his detractors have their say. To prove that he meant business he began to denounce openly the injustice of the system which divided Hindu Society into categories by consigning a group into an underclass and refusing them any mobility notwithstanding their merit and notable achievements. He made himself many enemies but as time went by he became more and more committed to the justice of his cause. He did not give up his belief in the basic orthodox way, in which he was raised. He thought that without carrying the label of any reformist movement he could still achieve his objective by example and by spreading education.

Pahlad made many converts. It took several years before his efforts started bearing fruit. In spite of the rebuffs he struggled on with the zeal of a missionary. Until his last breath he continued denouncing the iniquity of the caste system which had for generations corroded and weakened Hindu Society. Pahlad's memory is revered to this day in his village.

A street in a rural area. The inevitable sugar canes cover any available space.

A modern sugar mill with a capacity of over 50,000 tons of sugar. Lorries of sugar canes are waiting to be unloaded.

A typical Chinese shop in a village. They are fast disappearing, giving way to supermarkets.

A Chinese shopkeeper in his shop.

The Story of the Chinese Shopkeeper

In the thirties Mauritius still offered the prospect of a vast sugar cane field scattered with factories whose tall chimneys belched out sooted smoke for the three harvest months of the year, causing considerable harm to the environment. Around those chimneys villages had developed, attracting the Chinese shopkeeper always close at heel to exploit the retail trade.

A solid structure of stones and iron sheets with a verandah almost encroaching on the public road, the Chinese shop was normally situated at a street corner, a strategic vantage point to attract business. The verandah, which performed the office of a public waiting room, gave access to the shop proper where the customer enjoyed sufficient space to move about without disturbing the shopkeeper who was shielded from unwarranted intrusion by a wooden counter over which all transactions were carried out. The merchandise was stored inside and the only visible goods were minor haberdasheries arranged on a shelf. In a corner of the counter which formed a right angle was a glass case in which were kept open tins of sardines in oil.

The premises housing the shop also doubled as a residence. In the cramped space amid bags of rice and the smell of dried fish, wooden beds were fitted for the workers. If the shopkeeper had a family a small addition would be provided to accommodate the couple and the children. Badly ventilated as it was, with hardly any light, the Chinese family would manage to cook, eat and sleep in the limited space. After closing hours, while the elders would be busy preparing paper bags for the minutest purchases, the children would sit down with their books to do some homework.

Late in the night in the dimly lit backroom, the industrious Chinese would make ready for another day's labour to meet the demands of the most fastidious customers by making sure that all the consumables were ready for sale.

Alone in a shop, lost in the middle of a village composed mainly of Indian sugar workers and a minority of Afro-creoles, the Chinese had to display much patience, tolerance, discretion and hard work in order to survive. The shop was an essential part of the village economy. In hard times, especially during the inter crop, the underpaid labourers had to depend on credit to obtain essential commodities.

The shop was also the focal point of village life. Every afternoon after a day's work, young and old would gather for a drink and a gossip. As there were no radios and newspapers, rumours were freely traded and the gullible labourers would practically hang on to the lips of the village garçon who pretended to have the latest news. These rumours, however incredible, would percolate to the humble hamlets as gospel truth which even the sceptical, either overtaken by lassitude or too eager for news, would accept.

Towards the evening, the sundowners used to take possession of the bar and animation would then increase in proportion to their intake of rum. It was an interesting scene to see consumers gulping two or three tots at a time, alleviating the burning taste with hot salt cakes prepared in boiling oil in the shop verandah. As there was hardly any recreation between working and sleeping, drinking provided an outlet without which the workers could get bored to the point of committing reprehensible acts, even suicide. Sometimes drunks refused to leave the bar and had to be forced to depart by service being stopped.

True to his temperament, fashioned by millennia of Confucianism, the Chinese shopkeeper pretended to be indifferent to the noise of the gossip mongers by concentrating on his business highlighted by the rattling of his abacus. Yet he never missed an important conversation and was thus acquainted with what was happening in the village. 'Give every man thy ear, but few thy voice' was his guiding philosophy.

All over the island wherever the Chinese were established their behaviour pattern was the same, just as the layout of the shop which kept the same uniformity. The Chinese shop could be recognised from a distance, because its architecture was unique. It was a familiar, reassuring sight to cheer up the long distance traveller always guaranteed of some refreshments to spur him on. The village or any agglomeration could do without a school or a place of worship, but without a shop, the very lifeblood of the inhabitants was threatened. The shop was so intimately associated with the Chinese that any shopkeeper was assumed to be a Chinaman.

The shop I am talking about was situated in a small village in the south of the island. The story connected with it took place in the nineteen thirties, when the economy was very shaky and sugar workers were living in grinding poverty. The colonial administration had not provided any safety net by way of welfare to rescue the poor from total destitution. Labour law was unheard of and trade unionism a taboo. It was under these conditions that a young Chinese from Canton landed in the village to give assistance to the local shopkeeper, another Chinese known as *Longaille*, because he was tall for his race. As Chinese names were a secret outside their own circle, the inhabitants, especially the women who did the shopping, chose a name descriptive of the person. The newcomer was immediately christened *Gros Lisieux* (big eyes) because his eyes were not slit and looked big for a Chinese. The name stuck. It was rumoured that *Longaille* had destined him as a match for his eldest daughter, still at school. In those days, the Chinese, like other Asians, were very strict in the choice of partners for their daughters. No matrimony outside the tribe and the caste was tolerated. If a proper match was not available locally, recruitment back home in China was resorted to.

Gros Lisieux made very rare appearances at the beginning as he was kept busy undergoing a crash course, mastering basic Creole and the names of articles in regular demand by consumers. After four weeks he began serving small items and his broken Creole pronounced in a strong Chinese accent made him popular because he was funny. His youth and good appearance made up for his language deficiency. Before long, young men of his age wanted to get to know him because he was a foreigner from a far off country about which they wanted to learn more. As he was also keen to get to know them, friendships developed which helped him to speed up his familiarity with Creole. But he did not realise that he was breaking one of the golden rules of his peers, who did not encourage friendship with the locals.

Longaille especially did not appreciate his behaviour and told him so. But *Gros Lisieux* was too independent to be tied to the conventional aloofness which characterised the Chinese community. He was a sort of rebel but a rebel for a good cause, much in advance of his time. He began to accompany his friends to village weddings and other celebrations which gave him an insight into the life of the villagers who were predominantly Indian. He soon learnt Bhojpuri, the language of the local inhabitants and practised it on the womenfolk, much to the latter's delight. He had also a romantic side which appealed to the fair sex.

Gros Lisieux was gradually becoming unwanted for another more important reason. The plan of his boss to integrate him into the family had fallen through as the daughter had spurned the very idea of marriage by choosing a career as a teacher which was to take her out of her native backwater in which her father had destined her to carry on in the family tradition. It was welcome news to *Gros Lisieux* who was also not keen on the proposed matrimony. After this disclosure, *Gros Lisieux* had become more of a burden than before and since *Longaille*, his boss, felt no more obligated to him, he was summarily dismissed one day and told to leave the shop.

As a discreet Chinese, proud of his self respect, he did not disclose the news to any of his local friends. He simply took the train to Port Louis, where he booked accommodation at a Chinese Club. It was a meeting place for all the shopkeepers from the countryside who came to town for their weekly wholesale purchases. Some stayed for a game of *quatre quatre*, four by four or *Mah jong* as a break from the humdrum of their retailing activities. By now *Gros Lisieux* had perfected his Creole and knew also some French, enough to enable him to fend his way around the city.

It was at the Club that he met a shop owner much older than himself who, having only recently lost his wife, was desperate for a partner. He was a person who inspired confidence and could be trusted. He proposed to *Gros Lisieux* interesting terms such as food, lodging, a salary and also a partnership in return for a small investment. The latter who had a savings of Rs 500, a big sum in those days, readily accepted and without any more formality handed over the money and boarded the truck which took both of them and the merchandise to a very remote village, much more isolated than the one he had left. As a stranger in the country, he had no choice but to accept his destiny as it came. He was well adapted to the Mauritian style of life and had long discarded his percal national dress in favour of a Western suit. The prospect of finding himself stranded in a forsaken village with no social life made him gloomy, but he derived consolation from the expectation that it was not a life commitment and he could always liberate himself from the bond and seek fortune elsewhere. He had youth in his favour and in the Chinese matrimonial market, he was a valuable commodity. As a resourceful young man, as soon as he had settled into his new abode, he scoured the surroundings to discover those things that could sustain him in his moments of loneliness. His *bhojpuri* was most useful in helping him to establish contact. His arrival in the village had created a sensation. A new *commis*, a shop assistant, had come. He was young and spoke *bhojpuri.* The word went round and practically the whole village wanted to greet him. To his astonishment, he had become a hero. It was a beginning which augured well for his future well-being.

A few young men of the village, teachers, tailors and taxi drivers who had befriended him invited him to their social functions, such as religious ceremonies, Holi celebrations and even weddings. He renewed his old habits from his former village, habits which had landed him into bad feeling with his former boss. This time he felt more relaxed as his partner was more tolerant and had given him full latitude to spend his leisure as he chose. It did not take him long to find satisfaction in his new environment.

There was practically no activity during the day at the shop and he was free to meet his friends and even go fishing in the river. In spite of its remoteness and the limited local activities such as cane farming or animal breeding, the villagers were well to do. The houses were timber, covered with iron sheets and a glazed verandah as a show piece. Quite a few had lorries which were out throughout the whole day. In the evening the shop was crowded and although sales did not match the number of visitors, there was no demand for credit. Everybody had money and the business was not bad for a village shop.

Gros Lisieux was intrigued by the relative prosperity of the inhabitants. His inquiry of his partner did not elicit any satisfactory answer, it was a mystery which became obsessive and for his own peace of mind he resolved to find an explanation. None of his friends was helpful. The code of secrecy, like the Sicilian Omerta, was strictly observed on pain of death.

One day, during one of his excursions in the outlying forests, he heard some muffled voices and a strong smell of molasses. Far from being deterred, he followed the smell by walking gingerly to avoid rustling the leaves. After about half an hour of precautionary progress, he suddenly found himself face to face with three individuals who were so surprised that they became speechless and unable to move. *Gros Lisieux* was just as surprised with the unexpected encounters. But one of them, being suspicious of his presence, pointed a gun at him after regaining his composure and threatened to put a bullet in him if he did not reveal what brought him to them. *Gros Lisieux*, who thought that his end was near, pleaded that it was by sheer accident that he had come to the place. He was the village shopkeeper and had lost his way whilst taking a walk in the forest. He had not even for a minute suspected their existence. He added that he was new in the village and meant no harm to anyone. The three individuals seemed to be satisfied with his explanations but warned him that if ever he revealed to anyone what he had seen they would not hesitate to kill him wherever he would happen to be. They showed him the direction for his return journey and told him to depart and never to venture again in the vicinity.

Gros Lisieux was so shaken that before he reached the main road he was looking over his shoulder every now and again to make sure he was not being followed. He reached the shop still shaking with fear. He only felt out of danger when for a whole week he found no threat stalking him. Only later, when he came to know that those people were engaged in the illicit distillation of rum, did he realise his narrow escape from death.

He was shocked to learn that the village which he had begun to love and where practically every family was living in comfort was a den of illegal distillers. There was an artificial climate of well-being which was overshadowed by frequent police raids and the arrest of respectable villagers whose long absence in gaol never dented their reputation, but was rather accepted as a matter of ordinary routine.

The villagers were a monolithic group, so strong was their unity. The nature of the business in which they were engaged necessitated a code of conduct which left no compassion for whistle blowers. The punishment, when discovered, was instant death. Each household was armed with guns acquired illegally. The village had its own security system and no intruder was allowed to be too inquisitive. The grapevine telegraph operated with such efficiency that the presence of Police would be signalled long before the officers would start their operation. Even children were trained to spot out any unwelcome visitor, and transmit the coded messages, often using fire crackers. *Gros Lisieux* was conscious that if he had to live among them he must be like them and observe the rule.

After recovering from the shock of his encounter with the distillers, he resumed his normal life as if nothing had happened. He became more friendly with the people, always keeping in mind his alternative objective which was to move to the capital and try his luck away from the danger of the gun and police raids. His partner, who had resisted the temptation of easy money by selling the illegally distilled spirit, had decided not to take out any licence to sell alcohol just to be on the safe side of the law. *Gros Lisieux* had approved of the wise decision.

While he was daily cogitating on the proper occasion to move out, an unfortunate event happened which compelled him to put on hold his plan at least for a few months. His partner died quietly in his sleep without giving any sign of his impending end. In his will, he had appointed him as his successor. Overnight, *Gros Lisieux* had become owner of a shop. He came from a small village in Canton almost destitute. After only five years he was a man of means.

His star brought him luck. But the luck also condemned him to the village for an indefinite time, or at least until he could find a buyer to liberate him. But destiny which was inexorable in its verdict had decided otherwise.

Part II

When *Gros Lisieux* had first arrived in the village, a young girl used to come to the shop with her friends, not so much to make any purchase as to talk *bhojpuri* to him and pull his leg. She had a mischievous look and her body was showing signs of fast development, but her behaviour was very girlish. *Gros Lisieux* did not pay much attention to her at first but her persistent pestering sparked one day a response which took her by surprise. He had come out from behind the counter and holding both her arms shook her by telling her in *bhojpuri* to try to behave, otherwise next time he would give her a good spanking. While he was in the process of shaking her, he looked at her very closely and for the first time their eyes met. He instantly realized that he was holding the arms of a grown up girl whose eyes sent the love signal to which he could not remain insensitive. The initial violence gave way to a sagging motion and finally to a listless release. The girl ran away and disappeared. *Gros Lisieux* was now slightly shaken in his turn. What had happened transformed him completely. From that day on, the village became also his village and he sensed an affinity with the local people. The girl became his obsession. He was disappointed when he did not see her in the shop the next day and the day after and after. A week passed and he did not see her although he waited a whole day. Any person resembling her would immediately attract his attention only to end in disappointment.

It is important to observe here that after the death of his partner he recruited a Chinese assistant to help in the shop. He was also foreign born but had learnt the usage of the local language and customs after several years' residence. The main burden of running the shop was to be on his aide as *Gros Lisieux* absented himself frequently on errands to Port Louis or on his social engagements with his friends in the village. The assistant, known as *Moustache*, because he had a thin layer struggling to survive, was an astute businessman. Not only did he run the shop efficiently but he increased profits and reduced all wastage. The loss of contact with the girl almost sent *Gros Lisieux* mad. He lost interest in his shop and was so distracted that he could not give a good service to the customers. He absented himself regularly during the day when business was slack and the whole village was out in the fields with the exception of the old and the very young. He wanted to locate the girl and meet her.

The girl, after running away from the encounter with *Gros Lisieux*, was as disturbed as the latter. Something had happened to her which had transformed her completely. She would shut herself in her room and dream for hours. The object of her dream was no other than *Gros Lisieux* who had become her icon. She had moments of such paroxysm of happiness as to be tantamount to a height of blissfulness.

The mother saw the transformation and immediately sensed that she was going through the crisis of puberty and was on the threshold of womanhood. She seriously thought that the time was ripe to look for a suitable match and get her settled. As a first step she was forbidden to go out alone to avoid any malicious gossip. Secondly she was made to adopt the *sari* to give her the dignity of a well brought up Hindu girl.

Gros Lisieux in his search for her spent hours every day trawling every nook and corner of the village until he discovered her residence, at the end of a long alley guarded by a couple of vicious mongrels. In order not to arouse suspicion about his daily rounds in the village, he pretended to be looking for eggs and poultry which indeed he made a point to buy, so much so, that his assistant thought he was opening a new line of business.

One day he made bold to enter the drive, purposely to attract attention by provoking the barking of the dogs. He knew that the girl would come out and he would pretend that he was looking for fresh eggs. The plan worked to perfection. When the girl saw him, she almost lost her balance, but immediately composed herself and after making sure that nobody was around inquired coyly but with a streak of mischief whether he was looking for eggs for his new line of business. *Gros Lisieux*, who discovered that she was making an opening for conversation, replied that eggs and poultry were an excuse to meet her as he had not seen her after her last visit to the shop about five weeks ago. She explained that her mother had decided that she was grown up now and should avoid going out alone even to the shop in order not to give rise to unpleasant gossip. She had even overheard her parents talking about a suitable boy as a match for her. A visit had already been fixed to the boy's family to fix the date for the wedding. *Gros Lisieux* was most perturbed on hearing the news. He wanted to know her feelings. She said she was too unhappy and would rather die than get married to a person she had never met. She confessed that she had been thinking about him and was so pleased to see him. It was a sentiment which he swore was shared by him in equal measure and with deep emotion. They agreed to meet as often as possible but very discreetly. In the meantime, the girl's parents had set in motion the marriage arrangements. The engagement was fixed in a month to be followed by the wedding, invitations were issued.

Gros Lisieux, being Chinese, and the Chinese being known for their avoidance of amorous adventure with members of a different community, as a necessary precaution for the safeguard of their business interests, did not at first arouse any suspicion as to his conduct. Their oriental type of courtship lasted for a few weeks until the news of the impending marriage compelled him to take a fateful decision i.e. arrange to elope with the girl to a safe place among his own people. He knew that if the relationship became known his position would become untenable. He remembered the gun menace. Now his position was worse. Hindus do not like their girls to marry outside their caste. To cross the frontier into a foreign race was the worst crime against the sacred traditions to be visited not by ostracism which was too mild, but violent death.

Gros Lisieux was desperate. Either he had to lose the girl or risk losing his shop, because if he were to take away the girl, there was no question of his showing his presence in the village again. He was in a serious dilemma but he was in love and did not wish to abandon his happiness, whatever the price. He would not be the first one to marry an Indian girl. There had been precedents, which entailed a heavy price in terms of bodily harm and loss of business, but once the fact was accomplished hard feelings subsided and life resumed its normal course. He knew of two such cases in which the half caste Chinese children were adopted by the neighbourhood and were integrated in the community as Hindus, carrying the mother's caste.

As a typical Chinese, he never shared his intimate feelings with even his closest friends of whom there were a few in the village. He therefore did not have the benefit of advice in a moment of such deep emotional crisis. He had to act on his own judgment. His passionate love for the girl had clouded his capacity to reason yet he was aware of the danger involved. If he eloped with her, he would provoke the explosive wrath of the villagers who would give him no quarter for the humiliation inflicted by his outrageous conduct. But he had made up his mind.

Come what may, he could not entertain for a single moment the thought of his girl in another man's arms. When he met her next, he disclosed a plan for them to elope. On the appointed day she would walk out of her house empty handed, very nonchalantly and meet him at the junction of the road leading to *Quartier Militaire*. There he would pick her up in a private car to drive straight to Port Louis where he had hired a room in China Town. He had told his assistant he would be absent for a few days as he had to see a doctor and follow a treatment to his eyes which had reddened due to lack of sleep. He did not reveal that the redness was due to his pre-occupation with planning the elopement. The friend naively believed him and promised to look after the shop with the same sense of responsibility as the owner.

A Hindu girl with a Chinese in a private car would give rise to immediate suspicion. To avoid such a suspicion, the girl had discarded her sari in favour of a dress. She had let her hair loose and allow it to fall on her back. Her appearance could be that of an Indo-Christian or Creole which made consorting with a Chinese less objectionable. They reached Port Louis without any incident and, once installed in their room, they both waited for a reaction. The girl suddenly became aware of the enormity of her act and thought of her home, her parents, her brothers and sisters, her friends. All the memories of her life in her village suddenly crowded back and she was overwhelmed with remorse. She began to cry and it took some time before *Gros Lisieux* could comfort her by invoking the vision of a happiness waiting for them. After all they both had decided on the present course and there could be no looking back, the Rubicon had been crossed. She would not be accepted back by her parents and he would be exposed to serious threat to his life if they made the mistake of going back to the village.

In the meantime alarm was raised in the village that the daughter of so and so had disappeared. The theory of a suicide was quickly discarded because there was no justifiable reason for such a desperate course. She was happy and loved by her parents who had a comfortable life style, albeit from undisclosed sources. She was young and had a life full of hope and ambitions ahead. It was on the third day that it was discovered that *Gros Lisieux* was equally absent from the shop and had not been seen in the village taking his daily walk. The mystery was about to be solved. The partner of *Gros Lisieux*, when pressed about the latter's whereabouts, could simply answer that he had gone to Port Louis to see a doctor as he was suffering from inflammation in his eyes. There was great animation in the village. Speculations began to take all kinds of proportions. After the theory of suicide was abandoned, one possibility was left which gained credence very rapidly. The simultaneous disappearance of both *Gros Lisieux* and the girl could lead to only one conclusion: they had eloped and must be somewhere in Port Louis. Several people then remembered having seen *Gros Lisieux* often engaged in intimate conversation with the girl during the day time. His partner should know where to find them. His pretended ignorance was a strategy to hide the truth, no doubt he was in the secret from the beginning. An aggressive crowd gathered in the shop and threatened to kill him and set the shop on fire if he would not divulge the whole truth about *Gros Lisieux*. He protested his innocence and put himself at their mercy. He was a total hostage in the hands of the villagers. He looked at their faces and could find no sympathy in any of them. To save his skin he suggested enquiring at the Club in Port Louis where *Gros Lisieux* was in the habit of staying.

The shop was given a respite while the village met to discuss the problem which had assumed a serious social dimension as the reputation of a prominent member was on the line. The disappearance of his daughter had already shaken his standing. If it was proved that she had eloped with a Chinaman, his position in the village would become untenable. He would ultimately have to emigrate to escape the censure of the community and his rejection as an outcast.

There was in the village a new movement, inspired by a liberal reform of Hindu Society in order to get rid of all the supposed rottenness eating up the energy and the sap of the Community. The Arya Samaj Movement, which had made a tremendous impact ever since the teachings of Swami Dayanand Saraswati[1] were spread among the poor orders, had already found a good following among the inhabitants of the village. The new adepts were openly against the caste system and believed in the conversion of non Hindus. The rejection of caste removed the main obstacle of a place in society for the converts. But the activities of the preachers of reform, who were highly critical of the orthodox practices, had split the Community: they were only kept united by their common interests in illicit distillation. During the discussion of the disgraceful events which had shocked every household, two schools of thought emerged. One, the Reformist, opted in favour of a face-saving solution. In other words, a group was to go to Port Louis and persuade the lovers to accept a ceremony of conversion and a wedding according to the reformed Hindu rites. They would thus be forgiven their misdeed and be able to reintegrate their normal life in the village. The orthodox were scandalised and felt outraged by such a proposition. The lovers should be banned from the village to set an example to any would-be offenders. The shop should be boycotted and the partner of *Gros Lisieux* firmly told to wind up his business and leave. The village became divided into two violent factions. The situation was fast deteriorating and the risk of open confrontation was rising every day. As a compromise it was decided to consult some elders and submit to their views. The next day, a few prominent members, highly respected by both factions, were invited to arbitrate. Practically the whole village turned up at the *baitka*[2]: the discussion was both highpitched and a verbal battle

1. A great religious and social reformer and founder of the Arya Samaj Movement, a militant organisation waging a relentless battle against caste system and the inequity of gender discrimination.
2. The local club where members met to discuss the village problems.

interpolated with vitriolic expressions was being freely exchanged until one of the elders raised his stentorian voice and brought the tumult to heel. None of the two factions, he began, had the same interest in this sad event as the parents of the girl. If the father was present, they should listen to what he had to say and abide by his views.

The father who was present faced the most embarrassing moment of his life. First he was already demeaned when he had to face, on one hand a hostile crowd for the disgraceful behaviour of his daughter, and on the other a group of people, not so much intent on restoring his dignity, as to pursue their own religious agenda by inducing him to espouse their views which were quite unorthodox. After some hesitation, influenced by the love for his daughter, he rallied to the reformists and at that very instant broke with his life long traditions and with his peers to whom the reformists were a bunch of hoodlums pretending to rise above their station by challenging the age old sacrosanct hierarchy of traditional Hindu society. The triumph of the reformists was a watershed not only in the village but also in the district of the neighbourhood the consequences were far reaching. The traditionalists from that fateful moment felt resigned to the storming of their bastions by the Reformists.

The prohibition of intercaste marriage began to subside from that time, matrimonial relationship outside the Community was not countenanced but tolerated as an inevitable evil. Society was undergoing a radical transformation with the girls being accorded the same opportunities as boys for education and in their choice of partners.

The Wedding

After the parental consent was obtained, a group of young men landed at the Club where *Gros Lisieux* had established quarters.

The hostile feelings of the villagers had already been conveyed to him. He knew also about the latest development and he was expecting the delegation. The arrival of the young men among whom he recognised two of his friends did not surprise him. They reassured him and the girl that they meant no harm and that they were mandated by the villagers to make certain proposals leading to a normalisation of their situation in the village. They explained what had taken place and their efforts to find a solution. *Gros Lisieux* could return to his shop on condition that he agreed to be converted to Hinduism; secondly to undergo a Hindu wedding ceremony with the girl and thirdly to live in the village as a Hindu couple, members of the community with the children bearing Hindu names.

Gros Lisieux who was foreign born, having spent most of his time in the rural areas among the Hindus found no difficulty in agreeing to all the conditions. As regards the girl, she could find no happier solution.

The date of the wedding was fixed and until then the girl stayed with a relative, a few miles away from her parents' house. In the meantime, *Gros Lisieux* was converted into a Hindu amid a large congregation of the Reformists to whom even a good number of the traditionalists had joined. *Gros Lisieux* was christened Sudesh, derived from Suddhi, meaning conversion. On the day of the wedding, Sudesh was clad in dhoti, an Indian dress, plus a long buttoned-up coat and a turban. To complete the transformation brought about by the ceremonial outfit, a *tika*[3] was placed on his forehead and a garland of fresh flowers around the neck. Thus dressed as a Hindu groom, a procession of cars accompanied him to the bride's home where the wedding took place. It was the event of a lifetime in the village.

It attracted a large crowd and the fanfare that accompanied the

3. A small red or white dot on the forehead.

ceremony remained a golden page in the annals of the village. For years to come, the story was a living symbol of the progressive mood of a large section of Hindu youths. Sudesh behaved with all the zest of a new convert conforming, in the minutest detail, to the rituals of his new religion. His familiarity with *bhojpuri* helped considerably. His wife brought her contribution in equal measure. She was reconciled to her parents and they were both welcome members of the family. Gradually, the whole village adopted them and the children who were born out of that mixed wedlock broke the cycle of caste to start a new trend where merit opened the gate to the loftiest position.

Although he was a member of the local branch of the Arya Sabha, he and his wife never missed a religious ceremony at the temple. Every year he used to undertake the long march together with other pilgrims to fetch the *Ganga Taloa*[4] water for the *Shivaratri*[5] *Puja*. In his *dhoti* and *khurta* he looked a *pukkha* Hindu. He died at the ripe age of seventy, leaving behind a large family who were all absorbed in the community as full-fledged members. In the village his memory still evokes great respect.

4. A small lake in the upper regions whose water is considered sacred.
5. A Hindu religious festival in honour of Lord Shiva, a Hindu Deity.

~ The Gambler ~

Introductory Notes

Indian immigration into Mauritius did not consist of indentured labourers only. Several contingents of traders and skilled artisans also came as passengers paying their own fare. Whereas the traders settled in Port Louis the labourers were taken to the sugar plantations where they were tied to a particular estate and housed in mud hut camps. Thus from the beginning of Indian settlement two classes existed: one the sophisticated traders already possessed of some means and education, the other the sugar workers, almost all illiterate, having no skill to liberate themselves from the soil to which their existence was condemned. This division which dogged the Indian community for several generations and which is still reflected in their separate evolution, the urbans continuing their trading tradition and the rurals remaining attached to agriculture, has not yet been blurred.

The traders originated mainly from South India and a lesser number from Gujerat. In his interesting study of the history of '*Les Tamouls à l'Ile Maurice*'[1] Ramoo Sooryamurthy points out that the Tamil traders' immigration started immediately after the first contingents of indentured labourers. They were '*commercants et non des coolies émigrants*'[2]. Most of the traders were engaged in haberdashery and had opened shops in a wing of the Central Market, later spreading out their activities to other parts of the capital.

1. Tamils in Mauritius.
2. They were traders and not indentured labourers.

The recruitment of indentured labourers had been abolished in 1924 after a campaign of denunciation by Mahatma Gandhi and Pandit Madan Mohun Malaviya followed by a recommendation of Sir Kunwar Maharaj Singh, an Indian envoy to inquire into the iniquities of what Professor Tinker has qualified as a new system of slavery. But Indian immigration did not stop, they continued to trickle in as free traders and related occupation. The British India steamship company plying from Calcutta often offloaded small contingents in Port Louis. Some of them would later make it to Reunion Island or to Natal. Such a traffic was a common feature until the late twenties when an unprecedented world recession, of which Mauritius was a helpless victim, following the collapse of the sugar prices, brought it to an end.

~ The Gambler ~

The Birth of Samoondra

It was on board a B.I.[1] during one of its voyages to Mauritius that a baby boy was born to a couple travelling from South India. They were intending to go to Natal, but through some fortuitous circumstances they booked themselves on the first available ship leaving Calcutta and found themselves heading for the island of Mauritius instead of Natal. The birth of the baby boy was considered a happy omen which called for celebrations, but the limited space on the deck permitted only a small christening ceremony to offer thanks to the deities.

In those days the B.I. passengers who could not afford the luxury of a cabin had to travel on deck, making provision for their own bedding and food. The voyage could take a month or more and those passengers who could survive the rigours of the weather and the rough sea considered themselves lucky. Having a baby to look after only added to the hardship and severity of the voyage, but luckily for them, the young couple and the baby landed in Port Louis in perfect condition. The baby, who was added to the list of passengers, was named Samoondra, in remembrance of his birth at sea. In those days any birth on board the B.I. was only attested by a certificate from the Captain of the ship to be used for registration at the Civil Status Office upon landing. The father of Samoondra never bothered to report the birth and get a proper certificate so the boy grew up undeclared as to his status. How he

1. B.I. – ship of British India Steamship Company Ltd.

managed to join the Young Men's Hindu primary school remained a mystery. It was only much later, as the unfolding story will reveal that the truth was unravelled when he had to produce a birth certificate as proof of his age to qualify for his old age pension.

The parents, whom I shall refer as Mr & Mrs M.S. to avoid any reference, even an involuntary one, to any existing family, settled down in La Paix Street, Port Louis and through connection with friends from the same caste and province the father got a job as a store assistant in one of the trading firms owned by a well established Tamil family.

Samoondra grew up in an environment which ensured his cultural education and the preservation of his family values. He accompanied his parents regularly to the Mariamen Temple and observed the Cavadee fast. He even participated on a few occasions in the firewalking ceremony. He was not a bright student, he was just average and managed to pass his standard VI and followed without success the scholarship classes. That was the maximum he could achieve. The father had realised it was a waste to pay for further education by private tuition and that the best course would be to wait for two or three years when he would be old enough to get a job in the same firm where he was working. In the meantime Samoondra was left on his own. As there were other boys in the same situation they easily made friends and discovered that it was fun to go to Champ de Mars during the racing season and watch the horses in training and at the races. After a certain time they would bet among themselves as to who could identify the horses during training and name the winners. In this way Samoondra began to spend more time at the Champ de Mars and observe the horses and follow their performance at the training. He made friends with the stable boys and learnt more about the different category of horses, the distance for which each category was trained, their pedigree. He came to know the importance of the stable boys who had regular access to the horses and had studied their whims. The high responsibility entrusted to them imposed an obligation to see that the horses were kept in a safe condition away from any possible foul play. The animals were to be constantly under surveillance in order to keep them on top form for the races. Doping had not yet infiltrated the turf culture but the jockeys were not immune from the influence of the gamblers. Some were easily bribed to tip the winners. Not all jockeys were corrupt, the honest ones kept the bookmakers and the notorious gamblers at arm's length yet sometimes the unexpected happened. The favourite would lose by the neck or nose. The trick was to hold it just before reaching the finishing post, but on the whole punters were satisfied because foul play was not on a scale to warrant any outcry.

Before two seasons were out Samoondra knew all the tricks of racing. He could tell the fitness of a horse just by looking at it. He could tip with certainty the winners of the main races and his reputation as a reliable tipster soon spread in the small circle in which he moved. His passion for horses and racing was so intense that he would neglect everything to be at the Champ de Mars from early morning. He took no interest in anything else. As he had no money he could not bet but others who benefited from his tips recompensed him rather generously. In this way, although without regular employment, he was never short of money. Several times he tried to persuade his father to lay some money on a particular horse he knew was a sure winner but the father systematically refused. As a religious Hindu he knew the story of Yudisthir in the Mahabharata and how he was ruined in a game of dice to the extent of losing his kingdom and his wife. 'No one has prospered by gambling,' he used to advise his son. 'At the end of the day the gambler is always the loser. So be careful'. But Samoondra was living in another world. His prognostic did not depend on luck, it was the result of long studies and luck came into it as a remote possibility. If a horse was good and had a better track record it was bound to win. Where was the element of luck? Barring some unforeseen accident he could never go wrong. His father's philosophy was of another age and had no relevance to the Champ de Mars. The father discovered quite early after Samoondra left school that he was not interested either in an apprenticeship or a job in his firm. He thought that with time he would come to his senses and settle down in a steady employment. For the time being he was too young and should be left in the pursuit of his present passion as long as he kept himself out of mischief.

A bookmaker who had heard about him thought he could be of great assistance if he could brief him about the respective strength of the horses and their chances at the various races. He would be able to establish the horses' pecking order and fix the stakes. Samoondra thus got his first job in a field in which he felt quite comfortable. He remained with the bookmaker until 1943 when the Second World War was in full swing and the tide had not yet started turning in favour of the Allied Forces.

The war had brought fundamental changes in the life of Mauritians. There was rationing of all the basic commodities and everybody was registered and provided with a ration card. Young men were conscripted and sent to serve in the Middle East. The intellectual class had sailed to the United Kingdom to join the Royal Air Force and the lesser order enrolled into the Pioneer Corps. Samoondra, on the strength of his ration card, where he was registered as being over 18 also joined to serve in the Middle East, in spite of the entreaties of his aging parents not to abandon them. Samoondra was to be away for the remainder of the war and returned to Mauritius with his contingent by the end of 1945.

Even during the war racing events at the Champ de Mars had kept all their attractions as a national recreation. The Magalkhan where a few meetings were held at the beginning of the season did not offer the same spectacle, nor pull a large crowd. Champ de

Mars was the place where people from all over the island would converge for the big event like the Maiden Race, our national Derby, and the closing day of the meetings.

It might interest readers to learn that the Mauritius Turf Club, the oldest in the Southern hemisphere was established in 1812 and the Champ de Mars race course was inaugurated on 25 June the same year. Racing in Mauritius has a very old tradition and has influenced our culture so intimately that it is difficult to conceive life without it. It is so popular that every meeting becomes an event attracting people from all walks, not necessarily punters only. There was a time in the early days when besides horse racing, there were also pony races with the stable boys or lads as riders. Alexandre Dumas senior, in his famous book, *Georges*, delights us, with his usual humour, with a description of one of the pony races which normally took place on the last day of the season:

> Up to thirty Timur ponies would line up with the stable boys as riders to participate in the race. Hardly waiting for the starting signal, the nervous animals would fly off in a cloud of dust. By the time they reached Tombeau Malartic some of them would leave the track to take to the woods of Château d'Eau and in the process overthrow their riders. When the remnants reached Pope Hennessy Street another group would take the direction of the Cathedral, again getting rid of their riders. Only two or three would succeed in keeping to the track and making it to the winning post. The ponies which had strayed would regain their stable either late the same day or the next, chased by the street urchins. The public used to watch the whole show, with uproarious joy. The riders who had a rough time would limp back home, complete wrecks, with the risk of invalidation for a whole week.

The last day was also highlighted by other attractions among which the *Mat de Cocagne*, provided a hilarious entertainment The game consisted of climbing a greasy pole about thirty feet high, on top of which hung a prize comprising a man's suit, a shirt, a tie, a hat and a pair of shoes, all from a fashionable store of the capital. Several contestants, watched by a crowd offering spicy comments, would undertake the climbing only to crash down on the ground after a few feet. But before the end of the day when the pole had become less slippery after several attempts, the lucky contestant would appear armed with his cord and like an expert would succeed in reaching the top, waving the prize before dropping the items in safe hands to the cheers of the onlookers.

In the course of time the pony races were abolished, but the *Mat de Cocagne* was kept. The last meeting had become associated in public perception with races dedicated to sugar workers, because on that day they were given special leave to permit them to visit the capital and attend the races, as a reward for the end of the harvest. The workers and their womenfolk, who had made preparation for that special occasion months in advance, by paying for new clothes, flocked in droves to Port Louis by the morning train. As it was also an opportunity for sightseeing and making some purchases, their first destination was the museum and the Company's garden where there would be a stop over for a quick home made snack. The visit to the Central Market, for the much needed spices, would be left for later in the day, on the return journey to catch the train. At the Champ de Mars they would make their own contribution to the colourful spectacle by upstaging the dress parade into which female racegoers put so much effort. From the Champ de Mar they would spill over to the hills to have a better view of the scene below. The races themselves did not excite their interest. It was nice to see the horses racing along the track with their riders in multicoloured outfits but which horse won was no concern of theirs. They had taken no bet because that was not the purpose of their visit. They had come to the Champ de Mars to enjoy, to mingle with the crowd, to be able to tell their friends and neighbours they had been to the races and had seen the Company's garden and the museum, and bought good spices from the Central Market and the colourful sweets which they distributed to them.

Long before the races were over they would start the journey back home. Dishevelled in their crumpled clothes, exhausted by the day's heat, they would limp their way to the Central Railway Station where they would be huddled in small compartments to be rocked home by the coal stoked steam locomotives.

The urban population used to sneer at their clumsiness and bedraggled appearance. They were jostled at the station and since they were not in the habit of raising their voice in defence of their rights they were shoved into the train whether there were seats available or not. When they reached home they were happy and even displayed some pride when describing how the day was spent.

The association of the last race meeting, first with the Indian sugar workers and later with the whole Indian community, known as *Les courses Malabar*[1], began to carry a humiliating connotation. To many people, the massive response of the Indians to show their presence at the Champ de Mars on that particular day was a degrading sight, invoking an image of backwardness. We were still without any political rights and the workers were treated as chattels without any voice for their grievances. In those circumstances it was adding insult to injury to associate them with a sport with which they had nothing in common and which was invented to entertain the rich and the powerful. It was time to get rid of it and blot out that disgrace for all time. It was a big challenge because the task was to strike at the very citadel of power of the ruling class. Prof B. Bissoondoyal, who was known for his fearless denunciation of all oppression and evil which eroded the dignity of the Indian community, took up the challenge and by his systematic crusade to shake the Indians from their lethargy to

1. Malabar: a pejorative term to describe an Indian.

a sense of self-respect and dignity, he succeeded in a total boycott of the 1947 race meeting by the Indians, so much so that in a few years the mention of *Les courses Malabar* became taboo and is today buried in oblivion. As a protagonist of Indian revivalism at a time when the community was languishing without any hope, Prof. B. Bissoondoyal has earned a place of distinction among the great reformers of Mauritius. The war was over and the country was undergoing great mutation, both socially and politically under the impulses of Dr M. Curé, Sir Seewoosagur Ramgoolam and the Bissoondoyal brothers.

In the meantime Samoondar had come back from the army and resumed his contact with the races by obtaining a bookmaker's licence which, as an ex-serviceman, it was not difficult to obtain. He had matured and thought seriously of looking after his old parents and settling down after tying the knot with a girl of his own community and caste. He could not fit into any other occupation except betting on horses. It was his speciality and there his future lay. His stint with the bookmaker had given him plenty of experience but the rules of the game had changed. There were more horses in each race and more bookmakers too. More people were gambling. A certain amount of corruption had often crept in, the races were fixed in advance and the favourites were then the losers. He had to get himself initiated into the new rules and join in the game if he was to succeed. Horses' performance and form were not the decisive criteria.

The average Mauritian is a gambler by instinct. Gambling is indulged in at all levels of the social spectrum, the stake rising in proportion to the hierarchical status of the gambler. From a small bet the amount could rise to a substantial figure. Gambling was, and still is, a risky undertaking but because of the expectation of immediate gain the risk was considered worth taking. At each race meeting hundreds of thousands of Rupees used to be gambled at a time when the Rupee kept a respectable value.

Samoondra was lucky enough to have only a few rivals when he started as bookmaker. With his network of betting agents in the underworld and his relationship with the Police grandees built over a period of careful attention to their material frailties, Samoondra was in an impregnable position and could impose his rule, in defiance of the racing code.

With the jockeys as his partners in fraud, he could at least control half the winners at each meeting. He made plenty of money and became very rich according to the definition of the time. He changed his life style, bought himself the latest model of Vauxhall, a house in town and a bungalow at the seaside. He took as wife, a fair looking girl of the general population, who could act also as a trendy hostess. His parents had died and he felt no obligation to follow the family tradition of choosing a partner from his own community. As his wealth grew and he adopted the western style so did the retinue of hangers-on augment. Prompted by his wife he shed the company of his childhood friends to socialise with the upper layers, who were only too ready to oblige in return for the lavish parties to which they were the *invités d'honneur*. Every Sunday, either at his bungalow by the sea or his villa in Port Louis, the establishment, which included members of the judiciary, bank manager, race horse owners, politicians and leading members of the legal profession were regular visitors. Time was flowing so gracefully that few mortals could have been happier. The life of luxury with rich food and drink and the lack of exercise transformed him within a few years into a couch potato. He developed a big tummy, lost his hair, began to suffer regularly from gout, was breathless when making physical effort, and increased the sugar in his blood.

The display of his wealth and life of luxury aroused jealousy. Other people began to wonder why they could not penetrate his secrets and make a fortune. If he could bribe the jockeys they also could do so by outbidding him. Some new bookies who had joined the trade began spreading their ramifications in the racing. They first befriended the stable boys and through them learnt how the jockeys behaved to defraud punters. They also came to know how Samoondra was operating. In a single race he could make hundreds of thousands by arranging for the favourite horse, on whom large bets had been made, to lose. The betting public who studied the forms, the pedigree of the horses and their performance at the training and at the past races were often so sure of the result that they did not hesitate to risk a fortune on a horse. When to their big shock it was an outsider who came first they simply could not believe their eyes. Many people were ruined as a result of the fraud so brazenly committed by the jockeys with the connivance of the bookmakers. There were cases of people collapsing and dying of a heart attack on the proclamation of results for which they were unprepared.

The new breed of bookmakers who had come into the business decided to dethrone Samoondra, if they, in their turn, wanted to succeed. A few of them acting in unison represented a strength which could easily match the empire of Samoondra. By establishing a spying network they followed his movements, and those of his men, and the place of their meeting for the ultimate deal. By operating in clandestinity and making the appropriate contact they started by eroding the hold of Samoondra over the jockeys until, by outbidding him in their offer of rewards they succeeded in outwitting him and upsetting all his plans. Samoondra wanted to react but it was not an easy task. Sometimes the jockeys who misbehaved by accepting money from rival bookies were inflicted with mayhem, but because of the fraudulent nature of the transactions involved no report was ever made to the police. Gradually the newcomers began to assert themselves and they proved more than a match for Samoondra. He began to lose ground and money. The reverse process had started and now nothing could stop it.

But gambling is such a bug that once bitten you cannot get rid of it. Hoping against hope for a turn of fortune, he continued gambling because he had learnt to do nothing else in his life. Every year at the end of the season a dent was made in his bank balance. As the years went by he found himself compelled to sell his bungalow to maintain a semblance of his life style by continuing to entertain friends as in the days of prosperity. Before long he was bound to mortgage his house to pay for his betting debts. Since fortune continued to elude him even the house was lost. To his great humiliation he went to live in rented accommodation. His retinue of hangers on abandoned him, the high society in which he had thought he was investing to hedge himself against bad times turned their backs. Those who used to sit at his table ignored his request for an appointment, he had ceased to exist as far they were concerned, after all he did not belong to them. By accepting his invitation they had been doing him a favour, it had never been meant to be an act of friendship. They were having a good laugh at his pretensions, their message was clear to those who could read their behaviour. They did not mind sharing good food and drink, but that was all, the relationship stopped at the dining table. No erroneous interpretation was permitted – they were they and he was he – the line of demarcation had long been drawn. No overstepping was tolerated. Poor Samoondra realized his stupidity a bit late. He was abandoned by almost all those who had profited from his munificence. Even his wife, the common law wife, found it impossible to live with him in a rented house, with no maid to minister to her needs and no car at her disposal. Because in his hey day he had maintained a distance from the friends and relatives of his parents he was cold shouldered when he turned to them for some sympathy.

Abandoned, deserted, ignored, he suddenly found himself with no resources. All his savings gone he was not even in a position to pay his rent. Once the downward trend had started, a cascade of bad fortune followed until he was dumped at the bottom of the destitution pit. He became desperate and helpless but did not have the courage to put an end to his torture by a suicidal act. He even contemplated moving to a hostel to end his days, but he still had a remnant of pride and gave up the idea. How could he face the other inmates and queue with a plate for his meal? His last resort was to send an SOS to a friend of his youth whom he suddenly remembered and whom he had not seen for many years. In his prosperous days he had even forgotten that he was still around. The friend responded without the least hesitation and gave him shelter in his own modest dwelling, but the friend himself struggling to keep afloat could only help him for a short period. It occurred to him that he deserved to be assisted as an old age pensioner because Samoondra was, according to an assumed reckoning, already qualified. Samoondra then confessed that he had no birth certificate and therefore no proof of his age. He had tried to make out a case but the Social Securities people refused to entertain his application in the absence of an official birth certificate.

After racking his brains for a few days his friend decided to approach a lawyer known for his benevolence. He agreed to take up the case, provided two of his contemporaries could swear an affidavit in attestation of his age. As he was born on board a ship there must surely be some record of his arrival as an infant. After considerable research it was discovered that when his parents landed in Mauritius a baby was included among the passengers. This was an irrefutable reference. The proper affidavit was sworn and Samoondra was given an existence and a civil status. He then qualified for his old age pension. Being now less of a burden because he could contribute for his maintenance he was allowed by his friend a small asylum in a room.

Samoondra did not live long. After a few months he fell

seriously ill, the effect of his extravagance in his happy days, and he died one night in his sleep. He was duly cremated according to Hindu rites. A note appeared in *L'Express* notifying the date and time of his cremation and the place where the funeral procession was to start. Apart from a few neighbours and the family of his benefactor nobody showed up. He was cremated unwept and unsung. Thus ended the life of Samoondra known as The Gambler.

A village road.

A vegetable market. Mauritius is rich in green vegetables of good quality.

Horse racing is very popular in Mauritius. The race course in the Champ de Mars, Port Louis is the oldest in the Indian Ocean.

A sugar mill. Canes in lorries waiting for unloading.

~ The Drug Trafficker ~

Drug Trafficking is an abominable crime. From being confined to the few countries where the drug was produced, it is now so widely spread and so lucrative that the possibility of ever containing its damages recedes daily. The opium from which heroin is derived is cultivated on a large scale both in the golden crescent and the golden triangle. The coca leaves from which cocaine is manufactured is a vital part of the economies of Colombia, Bolivia and Peru. So far no adequate incentive has been offered to induce farmers of those regions to give up these lethal crops in favour of agriculture and livestock. The Americans, who bear a large share of the blame in aiding and abetting the cultivation of opium and coca in their crusade against communism, are now paying the price of their short sighted and socially destructive policy. By encouraging the insurgents against Communist governments to undertake the production of drugs to buy arms with the proceeds, they did not realize that they were creating a situation which would become entrenched and would continue to thrive long after Communism had ceased to be a menace.

In our time, drugs are a deadly social problem in many parts of the world. In spite of the severity of punishments involving death sentences in certain countries, traffickers through their widespread network, are more and more active and making fortunes which no other business can generate.

Mauritius, being within the proximity of the golden crescent, could not avoid being entangled into its web. The severity of punishment and the freezing of the assets of traffickers found guilty have not stemmed the flow of heroin into the country. Travellers from Bombay are used as couriers against the payment of a few hundred dollars. They take the risks driven by desperate poverty.

Dealers in Bombay have close links with suppliers in Karachi. If one follows the trail from Bombay to Karachi one discovers how the flow of heroin is facilitated by the link. Karachi is a distribution centre where merchandise from Afghanistan and the North West Frontier is smuggled in to be dispatched to the lucrative markets of Western Europe.

So far not a single courier from Bombay has revealed the identity of the importers or helped to trace any of them. The device is so ingenious that the real culprit, i.e. the godfather, is never caught. The courier is simply given the merchandise well concealed either in his body or suitcases and told to go to an address in Mauritius where the recipient would call to collect it. The person carrying the drug is never told for whom it is destined nor has he the means of finding it out. In the event of any indiscretion the person responsible can be punished with death. It is a business where the poor are exploited, the boss makes his fortune and where death lies in wait for any person who may be tempted to betray the secret.

Traffickers have such a wide network of informants that the slightest suspicion is reported and immediate precautions are taken. When a courier is caught, the news is released to the press by the informants who may be operating within the customs or the drug unit of the police. The courier is taken into custody, prosecuted, tried and sentenced to long term imprisonment, while the exporter and the importer, who are the true beneficiaries of the deadly traffic get away free. It is the poor courier who, for a few hundred dollars, takes all the risks and goes to prison. In some countries he can even be sent to the gallows.

Why is the whistle blown as soon as a suspect is arrested? Why can't the customs or police tail him to his hotel and keep an ambush until the importer or his agent calls? It is said that the system has been tried, but each time it fails because news is always relayed to the party concerned.

For the few couriers who are caught there are a good number who get through the net and the country continues to be flooded with drugs.

So far no measure has been found adequate and efficient enough to control the flow and the spread. The ravages it inflicts on our youth are such that now and then people wake up to the devastation, and demand stiffer measures to locate the real culprits, the godfathers as they are known in the underworld.

The build up of the drug menace reached its climax in 1985 when four members of the Legislative Assembly were arrested in Amsterdam on suspicion that they were carrying drugs. In the suitcase of one of them the stuff was found concealed. He was alleged to be the courier of an Indian trafficker. The public outrage that was sparked compelled the government of the day to appoint a commission of enquiry. Several suspects were examined and their assets and bank accounts scrutinized but again the godfathers remained elusive. A few individuals who could not properly account for their thousands in the bank were branded traffickers without any follow-up. The inquiry made some noise, a few senior police officers were suspended on the shaky evidence of a well known addict and street pedlar, who after a short period of public notoriety, went back to his gutter. Then the curtain fell, leaving the traffickers to have their field day.

But the mystery surrounding the big time dealers remained as deep as ever. Who were they, why they could not be unmasked? Suspicion fell upon some well entrenched in the establishment. But no one dared to point a finger because the suspects were too important, always moving in high circles protected by the armature of power. We were in the heyday of the mid-eighties when the country was blessed with a period of unprecedented economic prosperity thanks to Hong Kong investors. Some operators had become suddenly rich and were running two or three textile shops dealing exclusively in imports and exports. In addition, in spite of the increase in the cost of seaside property, a few of them became owners of bungalow complexes. They were regular visitors overseas to explore markets. Their sudden rise to wealth and influence created jealousy and their neighbours who could not feel comfortable began to talk and lead a campaign of gossip with ill forebodings. But the persons targeted were above their reach because they were too highly placed.

The *nouveaux riches* were most generous in their contribution to charity; orphanages and places of worship were the greatest beneficiaries. They were not sectarian in their largesse, any one in distress could rely on their assistance; several cases of children necessitating medical treatment abroad were subjects of their special attention; students in need often knocked at their door and never left empty handed; several widows and orphans were on their list of special help. Their charitable work and benevolence knew no communal or religious boundaries.

Some had adopted certain wards in hospitals to contribute to the welfare of patients. They were the patrons of sports, especially football, and several clubs could only survive thanks to their financial support. They were most vociferous in denouncing the drug dealers and joined in the crusade against the decimation of our youth. Some rehabilitation centres were practically run with their money. Their engagement in social rehabilitation of the deprived and the victims of drugs gave them not only respectability but also a popularity which left politicians miles behind. They managed to elbow their way into the society of the powerfuls of the day, were invited to all the important social events and were very conspicuous at certain official functions. To add credibility to their newly acquired status they would manage to be close to Ministers at the appropriate time so as to be in the press photo or on the T.V. They would arrange with photographers to be snapped when they would pretend to be engaged in intimate conversation with members of the Government of the day. During the Rault Commission of Enquiry it was revealed that certain traffickers used to make contributions to the political party funds and entertain politicians in return for police protection.

While the godfathers were taking society for a ride with their altruism, the tragedy in families where a son or a husband had been hooked on heroin and was descending to perdition leaving a trail of tears, was taking place on an increasing scale every day. The callousness or indifference of those responsible for the tragedy could only be measured by the magnitude of the ruin they had spread.

Ahmad was a promising young man who had just taken a job after leaving college. He belonged to a poor but honest and hard working family, living in a suburb of Port Louis, ill famed for drugs and drug related crimes. He had a weakness: football. He could not afford to pay the ticket and the transport to attend the match played by his favourite team. A casual friend, Garçon, who lived in the same street and ran a van, offered one day to take him to a stadium in the north where his favourite team was playing. The offer was too tempting to be turned down. His parents had always frowned upon an association with people engaged in dubious occupation and this friend belonged to that category. Without the knowledge of his parents he accompanied him to the match. After the final whistle the friend did not return to Port Louis, he took a road leading to a bungalow at the sea side in Cap Malheureux. He assured Ahmad that it would take him only a few minutes as he had to deliver a parcel. Once inside the bungalow Ahmad noticed the presence of a group of people, complete strangers to him. Instead of a few minutes the friends stayed for two hours talking about trips to Bombay, about women and drugs and similar matters in which impassioned young men indulge when they congregate. This was the first time he ever heard the mention of brown sugar and how it was sniffed but nobody at that particular moment smoked or sniffed any noxious substance.

When finally both left, Ahmad was disturbed by what he heard and troubled about the explanation he would give regarding his lateness, which was unusual. The friend dismissed his misgivings by telling him that those young men were harmless and the conversation was just mundane, not to be taken seriously.

He told his parents that a breakdown of the van was the cause of his lateness but he got nonetheless a good telling off and had to give the undertaking to avoid such lateness in future. His friend began to cultivate him with assiduity and tried to see him as often as possible. The football tickets and the free trips in the van were sufficient inducement to attract him. Gradually when Garçon was satisfied that a mutual trust had sufficiently developed he sent him on errands which consisted in the delivery of small parcels. He plied him with money which, in spite of his initial protest, Ahmad began to accept. He was inducted into the company of the same young men whom he had first met at the bungalow. His new circle of friends kept him until late from home. When rebuked by his parents he would retort that he was grown up and could look after himself. The parents soon gave up and tolerated his escapades. He soon found out that the small salary he was receiving was not enough to pay for the new life he was leading, frequent visits to cinema, football, restaurants, etc. He began to smoke and consume alcohol and quickly found himself in a position where the revenue from the small errands was important. One day he was persuaded to try to sniff the brown sugar. At first he was repelled by the effect but at the second and third try he enjoyed the nirvana it induced. Nonetheless he controlled himself in future and resisted the persuasion of his new friends.

He had suspected all along that the errands consisted in

delivering small parcels of drugs. Now it was confirmed that Garçon was a dealer and all his friends were not only sniffers but pedlars. It became clear to him why they were able to lead a lavish life style and he realised that he was going to be caught in a web from which it would not be easy to be released. After anxious consideration he finally determined to take his distance and shake off their company. But he had not counted on the sacrosanct code that once you joined the brotherhood of drugs you could only leave it at your own risk and peril.

Hardly a week after he had failed to respond to the call of his friend, two toughs arrived at his place of work and peremptorily ordered him to accompany them on pain of bearing serious consequences. He had no choice but to comply. This time it was not his usual friends that he met at the bungalow, but a middle aged man, in dark glasses who summoned him to take a seat with all the civility that he could command. After the exchanges of the usual compliments he told him that he understood his qualms but it was now too late to quit. He revealed to him that there was complete information compiled from his first visit to the bungalow to the last meeting with the group when he sniffed the brown sugar. He showed him photos of some of his errands and the places of delivery of the drug parcels. He warned him that the Police were fully aware of all his movements and at any time he could be arrested but he would see to it that nothing happened so long as he played the game by resuming his normal association. He was promised protection against the Police and financial security but if he insisted on acting the way he did then he would have to face the consequences. What they were was implied in the threatening language used. The last word of advice was that for his own safety and that of his family he should return to his friends.

Ahmad was completely shattered. He could not sleep the whole night and did not go to work the following day. He was tormented by what he was told, the veiled threat, the visit of the two toughs, his own vulnerability due to his exposure and above all the physical danger to which his innocent parents would be subjected if he now tried to distance himself from the group. He felt cornered, with his back to the wall. He did not mind any harm to himself but he could not tolerate anyone laying a finger on his parents. For their safety he decided, much against his conscience, to take the course he knew was fraught with peril and which could lead to his own destruction. At the same time he resolved to make the best of a bad bargain. He would join the society of the grave diggers to penetrate the secret of their evil network, to find the source of the scourge i.e. the godfather in charge of the drug trafficking. The latter was a mystery, eluding all description and keeping himself beyond the reach of the law. Ahmad resolved that he would atone for the evil on which he was embarking by helping to smash the criminal organisation while being part of it. It was a big risk but at least it was not a heinous course. If he played his cards well he would still, at the end of the day, come out with a moral vindication.

The second day he returned to the gang, apologised to them for his behaviour, promised his full cooperation and after some hassle was accepted into the fold. He was, however, kept under surveillance for a while before he regained their trust. During his probation period his sincerity was put to the test by being sent on some hazardous missions which required all his nerve to succeed. He was sent to collect drugs from the Bombay mules in the teeth of police ambush. He was also on a few occasions entrusted with a substantial quantity of the stuff to deliver at critical distribution points. He acquitted himself of all his errands with discretion, efficiency and speed and impressed everybody with his coolness. He never complained about his share of the proceeds. He had given up his job and pretended to his parents that he was engaged in the business of land and house agent which was bringing him more revenue than his previous employment. The new occupation permitted more freedom to visit his friends.

Thus within a few months he graduated from a simple pedlar into a gang leader in charge of Port Louis and its suburbs. He was taking orders from the boss he had met when he was thinking of defecting. The latter introduced him to some senior Police Officers under whose protection he was to operate. He also came to know the main distributors in the network: they were restaurant keepers, street hawkers, taxi drivers and freelance dealers, a whole regiment of the underworld known to police, who had done a few spells in prison. They were people who acted under fear because they knew any betrayal or dishonesty in the transaction would be repaid with serious bodily harm to themselves which could paralyse them for life. They were only two or three people in the chain of command, but they were forever conscious of an invisible power who could be ruthless. When a distributor was caught he never revealed his source of supply. The Police inquiry men hardly insisted, they had their quarry and that was enough. The media would give great coverage to the arrest but hardly bothered to query the identity of the true culprit.

Ahmad also was intrigued. After six months in the business he was still left in the dark as to who the big boss was. He was growing impatient and decided to make his own investigation. His reputation as a big time dealer was becoming known and he was already the target of all sorts of curses, he was branded the enemy of society, a merchant of death, whose company was to be avoided to be spared being tarnished with the same brush. He was conscious of his accursed reputation, but he could do nothing to rehabilitate himself, he had to continue in his disreputable occupation if he wanted to achieve his goal.

Although under protection of those police officers who were accessible to bribery he did not feel secure. In the force there were officers whose integrity could not be questioned. They would arrest him without the least compunction if he were found in any way to be connected with drug peddling. He therefore had to hedge himself against such eventuality in order to pursue his mission. Ahmad had to work his way into the confidence of these officers or at least the most trustworthy one. He was at a loss as to how to proceed. His best friends who were keeping away from drugs shunned his society. He did not know in whom to confide to enlist support to open the path to the officer who would believe him and give him the cooperation he badly needed. For several days he racked his brains for an answer. Finally he came to the conclusion that he could not trust anyone. The only person he could confide in was a Roman Catholic priest. Not that there was any special consideration to be expected from that order, the only guarantee he could expect was to be spared a denunciation in the event of the strategy being unworkable.

One evening he took his courage in both hands and went to the parish church and met the priest to whom he made a clean breast of his project and told him that it was now up to him to denounce him or to believe him and in that case try to help him. The priest became very much agitated. He was in a quandary. Ahmad had not confessed to him in the religious sense; he simply wanted his help. Was the priest to believe him or was he being taken for a ride? But then he thought, why should a man, a non-Catholic, come to confide in him and ask for his help for a goal which was for the benefit of the community? He took the decision to assist him and told him so. He had among his flock a senior police officer of high reputation, respected and feared because he belonged to that breed to whom duty was sacred and any dereliction a deadly sin.

A few days after Ahmad's visit to the priest, a meeting was arranged with the police officer in a small office of the vicarage. Ahmad was always in disguise and travelled in a borrowed car so as not to arouse suspicion. In the tête à tête between him and the police officer, the priest discreetly disappeared to allow them a free exchange. The officer wanted to be sure that he was sincere in his motive and wanted a guarantee that he was not seeking a cover to carry on his criminal activities. Ahmad asked for three months and if after that period he could not report any successful result the officer was free to act against him as a drug dealer. In order to report progress another meeting was arranged at the same place and the same time, i.e. 11.00 p.m. in two weeks. In the meantime Ahmad was to be allowed free latitude to carry on his business which he promised would not entail any abuse. He progressively reduced his trade volume.

The police officer also wanted to be on the safe side. He put his boss, who was the Commissioner, into the secret and told him in detail what had been discussed at the meeting. They both agreed to brief the Prime Minister and get his reaction.

The latter, who was constantly under heavy fire by the Opposition because of his helplessness to take stern measures against traffickers, saw in the information a golden opportunity to strike a stunning blow and thus retrieve the ground he has lost politically. He offered his full cooperation and strongly cautioned against the least indiscretion. He gave them a free hand but put it as a condition that a weekly progress report be brought to him by the senior police officer.

At the next secret meeting at the same place but after midnight Ahmad was conveyed the good news of the Prime Minister's positive reaction and was urged on to speed up his investigation before any suspicion could arise to put the quarry on his guard.

It was arranged for a meeting to take place once a week, each time at a different location and a different time. A password was to be used to facilitate communication by telephone in the event of emergency.

Ahmad had it in his mind that the real boss was the owner of the textile shops, the man who was projecting himself as a great benefactor. His inquiries led to the identity of Number 2 in the hierarchy. The latter was the manager of the textile import and export business and was in charge of the whole outfit. He discovered that the shops could not turn out profits large enough to pay for the lavish life style of both Numbers 2 and 1. People in similar business were complaining about the low turnover and the competition from the street hawkers.

In the meantime he had managed to increase his hold on the network of distributors and had even his own minders wherever he moved. The two toughs sent to intimidate him turned out to be cowards and wimps who, when they saw his rise to power, were afraid for their own safety. They transferred their loyalty to him after much apologising for their past conduct. Although Ahmad pardoned them and accepted to include them in his group he was contemptuous of them and gave them a status far inferior to the one enjoyed by the minders recruited by him. Emboldened by his new strength he told number 3 that he wanted to include both lower and upper Plaines Wilhelms in his fiefdom and insisted on having the deal ratified by his immediate boss. This was a strategy to ensure direct access to the latter.

Ranvir, who was Number 2 in the chain of command did not belong to the same community as Number 1, but he was his confidant and had the freedom to take decisions on his own initiative. He had heard about Ahmad and his influence on the distributors and his skill in avoiding pitfalls. At the very first encounter he was impressed by his self confidence and realised that Ahmad could prove to be more than a match for him if he chose the road of confrontation. It was better to come to terms with the reality of the situation and agree on concerted action.

Ranvir was a high caste Hindu, and had a sharp intelligence. He was always neatly dressed, custom tailored, and drove a BMW. He had moved from a small house in Stanley into a large villa with a long drive secured day and night by an iron gate. In the yard there were two vicious Alsatians the very sight of which was enough to scare the pants off any visitor. He had built up the reputation of a respectable man, never missing an attendance at the local temple for the religious celebrations and was known for his largesse whenever called upon for a donation. It was rumoured that he had connections with the higher echelon in the police administration and could, with his influence, get people either into trouble or out of it. He was ruthless with those who stood in his way. He was feared and hated but no one could lift a finger against him, he was a powerful man. His business often took him to Singapore, to Bombay and even to the United Kingdom on certain occasions. Every evening he had to report to Number 1.

Ranvir had made his debut in life as a taxi driver in which capacity he used to carry passengers to Port Louis two or three times a week. He was then living at Plaine des Roches. Competition was tough and he had to work hard to make ends meet. He already had a family, wife, three children and an old mother to look after. One day near the Central Market he had a dispute with a hefty chap, a lorry driver, who ordered him to move his car. A violent altercation ensued and in a moment of great provocation he dealt the fellow a fisticuff which sent him reeling to the ground. As he turned his back to go towards his car, another aide came with a knife straight at him. He was able to avoid the thrust by grabbing the arm holding the knife and twisting it so strongly that the offensive weapon fell and the fellow screamed for his life.

Back home he began to reflect on what had happened and became concerned that one day he might land either in prison or be the victim of serious violence. His trips to Port Louis became scarce and he changed venue from Central Market to Cathedral Square, deciding to look for another job. He was lucky to meet his childhood friend, Eshan, who had already a thriving textile business. He offered Ranvir the chance to take charge of his Rose

Hill shop. Ranvir was honest and served Eshan with unreserved loyalty. After a few years, when business was still thriving and the Comoreans were landing in droves to buy textile in bulk, Eshan decided to expand his business by opening a second shop in Port Louis. The loyalty and hard work of Ranvir had paid off. He was asked to take charge of the two shops and look into the import section also. He began to travel and during a visit to Karachi made the acquaintance of a rich trader and both became business partners. After a few visits Ranvir and Karim, the Karachi trading partner, became very close and conversation beyond the boundary of business, began to flow freely between them. One day Ranvir, acting on the request of Eshan, very casually raised the question of drugs which were finding their way into Mauritius from Karachi. At first Karim was unwilling to talk, but Ranvir very adroitly taunted him by observing that he could not believe that a man of his experience could plead ignorance on a subject which was the talk of the town. Ranvir wanted confirmation that Karachi was the home of heroin.

Karim explained that the stuff came from Peshawar and Afghanistan where poppies were openly cultivated as a valuable cash crop. Karachi was the distribution centre and heroin was easily available against dollars in the slums of the city but the police were ruthless with the dealers and often there were raids to track them down. He hinted that for the uninitiated it was dangerous to try to establish contact with the suppliers, who were mistrustful of all strangers whom they suspected of being police spies.

Ranvir had sufficiently warmed to Karim to win his confidence. He was persuaded that Karim could not be ignorant of the drug business, where easy money was to be made. He tried to strike a deal with him but Karim was as smart as Ranvir. He was prepared to recommend Taleb, in the slum of the Port area but he himself did not wish to get involved. He knew Taleb as a client of his shop, but could not say that Taleb was a trafficker. He simply conveyed that he might be able to help because he was a well known figure in the slum community. Ranvir was now in no doubt that Taleb was Karim's man otherwise the latter would not have mentioned him. Ranvir easily located Taleb and was given a warm welcome when he introduced himself as a friend of Karim.

After the preliminary civilities Ranvir mentioned the purpose of his visit. Taleb said he was ready to help, but he himself was not a dealer. He knew people who were in the business, but they were very secretive and would transact business only through agents whom they could trust. He could act as a go-between under seal of secrecy but an up front payment had to be arranged in dollars. Delivery was guaranteed in Mauritius provided Customs were cleared, any risk entailing loss of the stuff had to be borne by the importer. Ranvir told him that his boss, Eshan, would visit him to work out the mode of payment and delivery. He assured Taleb that Eshan was a man of means with connection in high circles in the Police and Customs who could be trusted blindfold.

In his weekly report to the Police, Ahmad did not denounce Ranvir, he wanted to make sure of the identity of his employer before blowing the whistle. He happened to know his name and had seen his mansion, but never had the privilege of meeting him. Beyond Ranvir the hierarchy was forbidden territory. No one could meet the boss. Ranvir was too loyal to his boss, Eshan, to get him involved.

Ahmad decided that the final act of the drama should now unfold. The risk involved to his own personal safety was too big but he relied on the discretion of the Police officer, to whom he revealed for the first time the involvement of Ranvir and the true culprit, the boss, Eshan. He was strengthened in his belief by the frequent visits of Ranvir, after dark, to Eshan in his mansion at Floreal, also by their business partnership, frequent journeys abroad and their expensive lifestyle. He insisted that their journeys should be checked and their contact in Bombay and Karachi followed, that was the only way to pin them down. Ahmad had been told by couriers, to whom he was often detailed to take delivery, that heroin was collected in Karachi and despatched to Mauritians, via Bombay.

The lifestyle of Eshan had already sparked adverse comments; his residence was a large mansion built on two acres of land in a well heeled neighbourhood of Floréal, high walls surrounded the property and a wrought iron gate gave access to a long drive leading to the house. Four fierce looking Dobermann pinschers mounted guard, their reputation kept intruders at a safe distance. Eshan received few visitors, and only by appointment. As he was principally concerned with welfare, his main activities were outdoors, he also owned a stable and his horses were often winners of the important race. He had an office in Port Louis which he kept for the sake of prestige but which he used only twice a week for a short period to meet friends and visit his stable. He was immaculately dressed and travelled in a chauffeur driven Mercedes. The salute of the beneficiaries of his munificence and that of friends and acquaintances was answered in the manner of royals with a slight wave of the right palm.

Eshan did not own any sugar lands, because, he used to say, he belonged to a family of traders who had long ago settled in Karachi. He traced his ancestry to the holy city of Medina. He used to claim that centuries ago, one of his ancestors migrated from Medina to Karachi to trade and stayed there, creating a family, which through the years multiplied and spread to different parts of the world. He held no proof except oral traditions which were sacred to him and unchallengeable. Unfortunately his ebony complexion belied his Sindhi origin. There was evidence, however, that his grandfather on his father's side came to Mauritius towards the end of nineteenth century as an indentured labourer from Bihar. He was a Hindu who converted to Islam, having fallen under the spell of a widow with some means. The father of Eshan who was respected in his congregation as someone who held a position in Government service decided to change his Hindu surname into a Muslim one by deed poll. Eshan, with his newly acquired wealth, wanted to go one step further by seeking a pedigree to enhance his status. His boast of an Arab lineage via Sindh, did not convince anyone but since no one dared to contradict him to his face he continued to dwell in his fantasy. It must be noted that Eshan never sought any affinity with the Surtees or Maimons, two exclusive Muslim communities often accused, perhaps unreasonably, of apartheid.

Not much could be found as indication of trafficking against Ranvir as he was officially travelling in connection with his textile business but the frequent movements of Eshan permitted the uncovering of damning evidence. It was discovered, by a thorough scrutiny of his passport, that from the U.K. he often paid visits to Bombay and Karachi, and his itinerary was also traced to Peshawar. In order to shadow him, the cooperation of the Drug Enforcement Bureau in Karachi was enlisted. An experienced officer was detailed to follow Eshan and find out his contact. At first it was difficult to identify him because he disguised himself as a native as soon as he left the airport. Without the cooperation of the Immigration, the officer concluded he would be wasting his time in a wild goose chase. Eshan had his contact in Immigration and a few top officers were on his payroll. Any suspicious move would alert him and he would simply vanish without leaving any trace.

The Pakistan Government was also engaged in tracking down the drug traffickers and although its intelligence had a thick file on the network and some of the notorious ones, it could act with success very rarely because the traffickers, who had a much more effective intelligence, were often tipped and thus were able to take precautions. Only the small fry and their accomplices who did not have ample means to bribe their way out were often caught.

The Immigration and Police in Karachi offered to help by trying to identify Eshan. This was not a difficult task as his arrival in, and departure from Karachi, could easily be noted. A plan was worked out by the Drug Enforcement Bureau in conjunction with Police and Customs to follow him on his next visit. As he was not in the habit of carrying any drugs on him he did not run any risk of being arrested. In order to forestall any tip off by Customs, Police kept a watch on arriving passengers, and as his photo has already been circulated it was easy to recognise him.

So on his next visit, a few months later, Eshan's presence in Karachi was signalled and, from the airport, without his knowledge, he was shadowed and every move noted. The hotel where he had his reservation and the taxi which used to drive him were carefully recorded.

Karachi is a big city with a very busy airport. It had for centuries been a great commercial centre. Now under the initiative of the Pakistani Government, it had developed into an international financial and trading centre. It boasts a large airport with regular air traffic from Europe, the Middle East and the Far East. With the development of business and employment opportunities there has been an influx of Pathans, Baluchis, Punjabis and descendants of Bihari Muslims who came to the city as refugees after partition and stayed there permanently. The result is that in Karachi the Sindhis are threatened in their numerical strength by the arrival of new fortune seekers. With the demographic explosion, several slums have sprung up, harbouring shady characters, thriving on drug trafficking and drug related crimes. Eshan was a regular visitor, during his sojourn in Karachi, to one of those slums near the harbour. Taleb, the contact arranged by Ranvir, used to send regular supplies of heroin to Mauritius via Bombay. The Bombay mules used to collect the stuff, and under pretext of visiting their relations, they did not find it difficult to obtain a Pakistani visa and travel to Karachi and back without arousing suspicion. The contact lived rather lavishly for a man of his station. In his two bedrooms in the port area slum he had a colour television, a powerful Yamaha motorbike and his cellular phone. It was rumoured that he had plenty of money but he preferred to live in the slum to retain his poor condition and thus prevent the wagging of malicious tongues. Eshan used to spend hours at Taleb's humble residence, often he stayed for dinner. In his disguise he was taken for a relation of Taleb. He never allowed the taxi to drop him close to Taleb's house but would always stop at a distance and walk. The taxi driver never found out the address of Taleb, although he knew the latter, having seen him in the company of Eshan in the streets of Karachi.

Taleb's identity had been traced by the Pakistani police and the Drug Enhancement Office. He was known to the police for his illegal activities but he always managed to avoid being caught. He was most mistrustful of police and it was not easy to get his cooperation. Although no evidence had been gathered to pin him down as a trafficker the net was closing in on him and he knew it. He had a son studying at the medical college in his final year before qualifying as a doctor. It was his ambition to see him as a doctor and he had planned to send him to the United States to specialise. Ultimately he wanted to emigrate after his son had settled in the States. The police knew about his plan and decided to blackmail him. An officer was detailed to talk to him with the promise of facilitating his son in obtaining a U.S. visa and even the green card provided he would lend his cooperation to entrap Eshan. The officer added that the police were aware of his relationship with Eshan, a Mauritian, disguised as a native. It was also revealed that Taleb was a drug dealer and he was using couriers from Bombay to send heroin to Mauritius and that Eshan was the boss whose network was responsible for the disposal of the drugs. The solution was simple: either he cooperated and realised his ambition or refused and bore the consequences as he would have to give an account of his bank balance, his life style, and his contact in Peshawar. Taleb felt cornered. He denied vehemently, at first, any connection with the drug world or any knowledge of the Mauritian named Eshan. He was given two Fridays to think the matter over. The parting shot of the police officer was the future of his son, the doctor. That was enough to break his resistance. He discussed the whole matter with his wife and made a clean breast of his heroin connection to her. As Oriental women are more sensible and more composed than their menfolk in such situations, she unhesitatingly advised him to cooperate. At the next encounter with the police officer he agreed to collaborate.

Soon a hidden camera was installed at his house together with a tape recorder. He was given strict instructions to behave towards Eshan at his next visit as normally as in the past. As was customary he received him, kept him for dinner and openly talked business. Both the presence and the conversation, which was incriminating were faithfully recorded. The police were satisfied with the evidence. He was next asked to inform Eshan that he was coming to Mauritius with his family for a holiday, and he would bring with him 5Kg of heroin for which he needed a down payment. Eshan advised against it, as he would be taking a big risk but Taleb assured him that as he would be travelling with his family and as it was his first trip no suspicion would be attached to him. Besides he would book in at a five star hotel. Taleb was talking with assurance because he was only carrying out police instructions and the SSR airport customs and police had been advised to give him necessary clearance as part of a big operation to which he was collaborating. His description and that of his wife and a young daughter had been signalled. As Eshan was unaware of the stratagem he gave his consent rather reluctantly and even promised to visit him to take delivery if nothing happened to him at the airport.

Everything worked according to plan. When Taleb reached his hotel the first thing he did was to ring Eshan. To avoid the leak that they were old acquaintances Taleb told him that his name had been given to him by a common friend who happened to be the manager of the hotel in Karachi where Eshan used to stay. It was a pre-arranged code. A meeting was fixed in Taleb's hotel room the same day. Eshan, mistrustful as ever, took Ranvir with him in case the parcel had to be taken charge of. Plainclothes police officers lying in wait had followed the telephone conversation and were ready for action as soon as the two visitors entered the room and settled down to talk business. Ranvir had brought the dollars to pay for the balance. Taleb had insisted with Eshan on dollars because he wanted hard currency to send his son to the USA. The heroin parcel was verified and Ranvir took possession. At that moment a loud knock at the door was heard. The three of them were given no time to react when the door was forced open and three plainclothes policemen appeared. Both the money and the heroin were seized. They were so stunned that they were speechless. They just looked at each other and allowed themselves to be handcuffed. Without anyone noticing they were taken out through a side entrance and put into two waiting cars which headed straight for the Line Barracks in Port Louis. On the way Eshan cried his innocence pretending that he visited Taleb at his request and he did not know that Ranvir would be present. He did not know anything about the transactions although he agreed that a parcel was given to Ranvir by Taleb. He did not notice any payment. He repeated the same story in presence of his lawyer. It was only when he was confronted with the picture of his visit to Taleb in Karachi and his conversation concerning the regular supply of heroin delivered by the Bombay mules and the proposed visit of Taleb himself that he became overwhelmed and had no explanation. It then dawned on him that he had been trapped and Taleb had played the main part in getting him in that net. Taleb became a state witness and was released on condition that he should not leave the country but make himself available to appear as a court witness. Ranvir confessed that he acted under orders from Eshan.

Pending the trial which did not start for three months, Taleb's wife and daughter were sent back to Karachi and he was given Police protection. But as neither Ranvir nor Eshan were allowed bail, their whole organisation disintegrated and the dealers employed by Ranvir simply melted without trace. The only man who was jubilant but completely ignored for his vital role in helping to dismantle the whole network was Ahmad. He kept a low profile and turned over a new leaf. After the case was over Taleb was put on a flight and sent back to his country. The money was forfeited and he returned empty handed but his son was given the visa for the US to pursue his studies.

Both Eshan and Ranvir had their property seized. Great publicity was given to the case. The man who used to denounce trafficking and drug dealers, who contributed to the rehabilitation of drug victims, and who was always in the company of the powerful of the day and who was present at every official reception, who was the owner of a stable which had trained several winners, was now behind bars for many years. The establishment was shaken and people began to look askance at the *nouveaux riches* who still edged their way into high society to obtain sanction for their wealth by the accolade of the establishment.

~ Gaston ~

The Night Vigil

Gaston had died at the age of seventy-two in the year 1960. He used to boast that he had known two World Wars, the Spanish Influenza, the demise of the Mauritius Railways and the dark days of the thirties when the price of sugar had plummeted to its lowest level, putting the economy on the verge of ruin. He had left behind four children and three grandchildren, all living in a large compound in the outskirts of a town, an inheritance which symbolized his hard work and a sense of family.

He died because the wear and tear of old age did not permit him to continue living. Until the last day he was seen in his yard shuffling around, admonishing his grandchildren for indulging in horse-play and making noise. No one in the family could have imagined that the end was near. After the death of his wife, Odette, two years ago, he was not the same person. This loss of his lifetime companion was too much to bear but his indomitable spirit had refused to give in.

A small malaise had precipitated the end. He was lucky to be surrounded by his family and receive absolution from the local priest before he took his final leave.

When the news of his death spread, a large concourse of relations and friends made their way for their night vigil where rum and black coffee flowed freely. Until the early hours of the morning people kept awake by playing games of cards and dominoes. In keeping with his wish he was buried in the cemetery of Mahebourg where his father, mother and only sister were laid to rest. The church service was well attended and the funeral procession included several cars and a coach.

Gaston, a black Creole, definitely belonged to a sturdy race of African origin. There was no written record of people like his forebears, who were brought as slaves to Mauritius by the French settlers in the early eighteenth century; they had no name and no identity. Slaves were not supposed to have history or identity, all links with their past being severed they were made to adopt the religion, language and customs of their masters. They were given new names, often to reflect the day of their christening or the description of their occupation. Gaston's patronymic name was Robuste, most probably derived from the sturdiness of his African ancestors. As they had no link with their past and no culture or history of their own to fall back upon, these people of African descent staked their faith in the soil of Mauritius and adopted it as their own homeland. The arrival of Indians found them well established with a strong bias towards skilled trades and as fishermen along the coast.

Gaston was born on a sugar estate in the last century, in 1888, and had no opportunity of going to school for the simple reason that the nearest one was four miles away. From an early age he used to accompany his father to the factory where the latter was employed as a carpenter. Before he was fourteen he knew enough of the trade to be apprenticed to his father on a monthly wage of Rs 10 plus some food rations. After his father's death he was given his job at Rs 30 a month plus a ration of rice, pulses, salt etc. and accommodation. His mother and sister were his dependents. His industriousness and sense of responsibility had come to the attention of the manager who gave him land to cultivate as metayer. Although he belonged to a community which had no reputation as cultivators of land, still associated with slavery in their mind, he made it his duty to take full advantage of the facilities available.

With his own and hired labour he first planted cane on two acres and gradually increased to five acres. In the interline he cultivated food crops. At the end of the year, favoured by climatic conditions, he made good profits, a windfall for which he had not budgeted. He put all the money in a savings account and never allowed himself any unnecessary extravagance. The Indian labourers who were engaged in similar occupations outside their working hours were his role models. Some had bought land in the adjoining village and built their own houses to which they had moved, others who were keeping cows and cultivating metayer[1] lands soon become planters in their own right. Gaston led a very sober life, rarely joining his peers on Saturday evenings for drinks in the bar of the estate shop. Although illiterate, he was very religious, regularly attending church. His friends and neighbours suspected him of being a man of means although he took care to avoid any display to confirm the suspicion.

His mother, who was getting old, and his sister, who preferred spinsterhood to marriage because of her poor health, persuaded him to choose a partner and create a family. He had found a girl to his liking, living on the same estate and whom he had met at church. She was the daughter of the head mechanic and was known for her mild and gentle disposition; she was also very religious, never missing the Sunday service. She had joined the Legion of Marie and gave a lot of her time to charity work among the poor of the parish. As was the custom in those days she had given up school after her primary school certificate and was attending a sewing class run by the nuns. Gaston could not have a better match than Odette, but shy as he was, he hesitated for many months before formally proposing to her. She was neither affirmative nor negative in her reply. She very kindly suggested that her father should be consulted. The father's consent was not

1. A planter who shares his crop with his landlord.

difficult to obtain as he was certain that his daughter would be in the hands of a very caring man, and a teetotaller to boot. It was also no secret that he had savings at the bank.

The wedding took place within six months of the engagement and excesses being avoided, both the church ceremony and the reception that followed were remarkable by their high standard and decorum. The wedding guests composed of an assortment of the estate workers had started preparations for the occasion as soon as the invitations had reached them. The tailors of the adjoining village had to put in extra hours to cope with the sudden surge of made-to-measure clothes. The older generation had dredged out their old costumes to get rid of the musty smell in readiness for the great event. They managed to fit into them although they looked somewhat gauche.

Well groomed and accompanied by their spouses in their new hats, both the old and the new generation made their way to the church in hired taxis. When the Manager of the Estate, the guest of honour, entered the church, everybody stood up and bowed. After the service, the Manager offered his congratulations to the new couple and left, the other guests gathered at the estate recreation hall for the reception. Although drinks were served, nobody was drunk. There was music by the local band and several couples took to the floor for a waltz. A self-imposed discipline had characterised the behaviour of the guests, the reception ended at about midnight and everybody retired very happily.

Gaston was congratulated on his choice. It did not take long for his bride to be completely integrated into the family. Odette brought him luck because a few months later he bought half an acre of land on the outskirts of Quatre Bornes where he planned to settle down after building his house.

The Manager of the Estate where he was working was fond of hunting and had hunting land of several hundred acres in the region of Midlands. Gaston had built the hunting lodge and a few miradors for which the Manager was most grateful. Part of the hunting ground surrounded a plot of twenty acres of land which he had always intended to get rid of. He proposed to sell it to Gaston for a small amount. It abutted on the extreme limit of Midland's village on its western side. The lands of Midlands were not fertile, too much rain had leached the soil by removing the top organic layer with the result that very few crops could be cultivated. At best some bananas, creepers and pine trees could be grown. Gaston, with his usual foresight and business acumen, saw in the land a plus value by the extension of Midlands village where the population was growing fast. He was convinced that one day he would realize big profits by parcelling it out. He readily accepted the deal as an investment for the future. When he bought the land in 1930 he paid only Rs 1000 the market price in those days of depression.

In the meantime, his family had increased by the birth of two boys and two daughters, his mother and sister had died. Having missed school himself he saw to it that his children did not remain illiterate. When they reached school age he had already moved to his house in Quatre Bornes. In those days, before the Second World War, the completion of primary education was considered sufficient for people of the class of Gaston, secondary education being a luxury out of their financial reach. After leaving school the boys were apprenticed, Jean to a mechanic, the younger, Paul, to a cabinet maker. Of the two daughters one became a nurse and the elder one a seamstress. By the time the boys had reached 18 the Second World War was declared. Mauritius, being a British colony, was inevitably involved, and several young men were recruited to serve in the army. The better educated ones, with a good knowledge of English, were enrolled in the Air Force and the less educated ones, like Jean and Paul, joined the Pioneer Corps. They were 23 and 21 respectively when they sailed for Egypt. It was a heart-rendering scene to see them being torn from their parents to embark on an adventure, the outcome of which, in 1940, was so uncertain. People who went to war had to fight and in the process could get killed.

On the day of departure thousands of parents, wives and fiancées came to Port Louis to say goodbye to their beloved ones. It was a magnificent sight to see the boys marching to the sound of military music through the streets of Port Louis on their way to the harbour. Although they looked alike in their uniforms, several of them were spotted, and their names were called out. The crowd did not disperse until the ship taking the soldiers to the battlefield faded on the horizon and parents and wives returned home in tears to spend their days in prayer for the safe return of their sons and husbands.

Thousands of young Mauritians had answered the call of the British Government and a good number never returned. Jean and Paul were among the lucky ones who came back after the German capitulation in 1945. The departure of a large number of young men had depleted the essential services of the much needed workforce. Those who came back from the war were given priority for employment provided they could satisfy the minimum criteria. Jean was accepted in the Police Force without difficulty and Paul took employment as a cabinet maker in the prisons with the rank of Prison Warden. Of the two sisters one was married to a car mechanic. Even so all the grown-ups resided under the same roof under the patriarchal authority of the father, even the son-in-law was brought into the fold. When the two young men, Jean and Paul, married in their turn in 1950 they were given accommodation in additional rooms to the main building. Gaston would not hear of any of his offspring setting up house beyond his purview, the land was large enough for all of them.

When the boys were still young Gaston used to take them to visit the land in Midlands. An attempt to cultivate bananas had to be abandoned because of predators. Tempting offers to sell were also turned down. In his wisdom he had thought of leaving a capital which could one day be put to the benefit of his children or grandchildren.

Afflicted by the absence of his boys, he had neglected his regular visits to Midlands during the war days. Even after their return he was rarely seen on his land nor did any of the children take much interest except for an occasional trip. As he was growing older he was persuaded by them to take a rest, especially after the death of his wife, Odette. For a man of his temperament who had been active all his life, rest was not a welcome companion to his health, he had to keep busy to preserve himself in good shape, rest was the final straw which shortened his days.

Of all the brothers and sisters only Paul had three children, two boys and a girl. The eldest one, Ernest had inherited the character of his grandfather, Gaston. He was orderly, neat and applied seriously to his studies. He always scored good marks at his examinations, so much so that his teacher had singled him out to be among the ten best at the Certificate of Primary Education examination. In fact, his performance was so excellent that he came out fifth in the island-wide competition. The result was acclaimed with big celebrations in the family. For the first time a member was going to the Royal College, the prestigious institution accessible to the brightest students only. His grandfather would have been so proud. Who could now pretend that children of the background of Ernest did not have the potential for intellectual achievements as good as any in the country? If they had lagged behind and seemed resigned to limit their ambition to the acquisition of manual skills only, the parents were to blame for failing to provide the opportunity to develop their talent.

> 'The fault, Dear Brutus, is not in our stars, but in ourselves, that we are underlings.' (Shakespeare: *Julius Caesar*)

Yes, the black Creoles underestimated themselves by regarding intellectual pursuits beyond their province. That was the subject of conversation in Paul's family and among friends and neighbours. They were all very proud of Ernest who had broken the myth of genetic inferiority. Fortunately all the fuss about his success did not go to his head. He remained cool and somewhat indifferent to the praise lavished upon him. It was again Gaston's gene which was active in him, but some of the remarks made by the elders regarding the inferior status of the people with whom he identified by affinity of blood and race had left a deep scar which stayed with him for the rest of his days.

When he went to college, he felt a sense of isolation and frustration because he could not make friends. From the first day a bond had developed among students from a common background. Thus the coloured, the Hindus, the Muslims, the Chinese and the Franco-Mauritians each formed separate groups. The student fraternity was a myth. In the playground communication between the different bodies was very rare, only certain sporting events broke the barrier. Ernest could not find his own kind with whom to associate, he felt lonely and only after a few months did he make friends with a few Hindu and Muslim boys. His social condition did not allow him to join the company of the well-heeled from Rose Hill and Quatre Bornes. Very early in his student career he realised that if he wanted to be noticed and make friends he had to overtake the rest of them by his academic performance; there was no half measure in this world of merciless competition. To make up for the deficiency of his birth and class, he had to prove that he was capable of equal, if not, better achievements than his classmates. It was the first of the many challenges he had to confront in his eventful career. His father did not have sufficient means to pay for private tuition, his earnings as a prison warden did not allow such luxury. Like his brother, the Police Constable, he was considered not qualified enough to deserve a promotion. His primary school certificate had lost its value in the face of competition from Cambridge School Certificates. Had it not been for the war he would not have obtained his job.

So Ernest had to persevere without the benefit of extra tuition. Notwithstanding that disadvantage he invariably ranked second or third in his class. He burnt midnight oil for a whole year to win the state scholarship for university studies in the United Kingdom. He just missed it; his ambition to do medicine and qualify as a doctor was shattered. Those were the darkest moments and he could find solace nowhere. There were no offers of scholarships by foreign benevolent countries for the six year studies which medicine demanded and his father could not afford the necessary finance. He cursed his star for being born in a poor family and envied some of his school friends whose parents had made enough savings to pay for their university education. The Indians and the Chinese planned for the long term and were keen to invest in education.

Ernest refused to be consoled by his father who tried to argue that with his qualifications he would get a secure job in Government and that not everybody had the good fortune of ending up as a professional. Ernest looked at him and said in a tone that surprised his father: 'Why should I accept defeat, attributing it to fate? I am going to fight my way to achieve my ambition no matter how narrow the gate through which I have to pass. It is the lack of determination to rise above our station that has consigned us to the margins of development. We have the talent, the capacity and the intelligence which are exploited for the benefit of others. We build houses for others to live in. We repair cars for others to drive. After cyclones we become homeless and take refuge in schools and welfare centres and queue for Central Housing Authority accommodation. We are absent in Government administration and in the business sector. There is a general feeling that our people are fit only to be watchmen and dock workers because we have the reputation of being brawny and not brainy.'

The words had the effect of a severe jolt on Paul who seemed to wake up from a long lethargy. He began to see reality around him, a reality to which his eyes were not accustomed until now. He did not utter a word in reply but quietly retired into his room to meditate on what he had just heard. Fully aware that his són had a strong character and would not flinch before any obstacle to pursue his ambition, he made it his preoccupation to find the ways and means of helping him. There was only one solution and that was to sell the land at Midlands to finance his studies. As it was still in a trust, he had a family meeting to get everybody to agree to sell either the whole or a portion of it. The price of land, as foreseen by Gaston, had appreciated and many people in the Midlands had made offers to purchase even small portions for residential use. There was an agreement on a division in kind among the four heirs. Ernest was elated at the news and knew that his uncle, Jacques, and his two aunts would unhesitatingly bring their contribution in case the share of his father would turn out to be inadequate to cover his studies.

Jacques and Paul, one morning, accompanied a surveyor to carry out the survey of the land and to proceed with the division. Great was their surprise when the watchman of the adjoining hunting ground with a rifle slung across his shoulder appeared and forbade them to set foot on the property. A discussion ensued which could have turned violent had it not for the intervention of the surveyor. The watchman claimed that the land was part of the hunting ground and his boss, the landlord, had given strict instructions to keep trespassers out. Dispirited and downcast the two brothers returned home to consult their sisters about the next step. The surveyor had advised taking the matter to court as it was clear that the owner of the hunting ground was claiming the land as his own for having prescribed it. It must be pointed out that after the death of the Manager who had sold the land to Gaston, the hunting ground had changed hands and a new owner had taken over. The latter had been in occupation since 1935.

Ernest, who learnt the news, was incensed. How could an owner with title deed lose his land to another person without any right? It was tantamount to highway robbery. It should not be tolerated. After consulting a lawyer the four heirs decided to go to court to claim back possession of their land. It took about two years before the case came for trial before a judge of the Supreme Court.

The Trial

The brothers and the sisters had contributed to pay the solicitor and the barrister. It had cost them almost a fortune but the land was too valuable to lose. Besides, it was an inheritance from their father who would turn in his grave if his children neglected to protect their property. The case had been entered against the new owner of the *Chassé*, a man of means belonging to the white aristocracy. A *chassé* to people of that class was a status symbol which provided opportunities for big hunting parties where important business was transacted. The Robuste Clan was going to cross sword with a powerful personality whose class had rarely known defeat in litigation. That person was known to all and sundry by his first name, Jerôme, to which Monsieur was a mandatory prefix. Monsieur Jerôme had retained the services of the best Q.C., Mr B. White, to defend his case.

Of the four members of the Robuste clan, only Jean, a policeman, was familiar with the court, being often posted for duty during the sittings. However, he was only accustomed to the atmosphere of the district court where the solemnity did not have the same rigour as in the Supreme Court. The other three had never set foot in a court of law. Their first day at the Supreme

Court filled them with awe and apprehension; the sight of a silent crowd in the public gallery, the hushed conversation of the court officers in their alpaca jacket and the row of barristers in their flowing gowns put them ill at ease.

When the case was called by the usher, they all stood up and their barrister, Mr P. Black, announced that he was representing the plaintiffs i.e. the Robuste group. Monsieur Jerôme also was on his feet and made a deep bow to the Judge who responded with equal courtesy. The declaration of Mr White that he was appearing for the defendant was made with a flourish that impressed M. Jerôme who was beaming in his seat. Mr Stewart was more solemn and in a grave tone opened his case by calling Paul to explain how he and his brother and sisters were the lawful owners of the land under litigation.

In spite of a ceiling fan, Paul was already perspiring and started his evidence in a shaky voice. He could not be very precise about the date of his father's death, until he was rescued by the production of his death certificate. Among the property left in inheritance he forgot Quatre Bornes where they were all residing. The Judge began to lose patience and rebuked him for his fumbling voice and loss of memory. Finally, the title deed of the land in Midlands was produced, the centre piece in the case for the plaintiffs. It came out in his examination that the *chassé* was fenced but not the land in question.

It was the turn of Mr White, Q.C, to cross examine him. Paul, who, in the meantime, had regained his composure, spoke with confidence and stood the gruelling questions without flinching. His lawyer was happy with his performance. He spoke Creole to be at ease.

After recess Mr White resumed his cross examination, with some aggressiveness this time. He began by asking whether he knew the land well, the acreage and the boundaries. Paul was not fully conversant with all the details but he did insist that he had visited it several times both during his father's time and after his death. He was then asked why they did not cultivate it. The explanation that the land was infertile did not satisfy the Judge. In the next line of cross examination Mr White wanted to establish that the land had been abandoned for over thirty years before the case was entered. Paul again insisted that it was not so. The land had never been abandoned.

The Q.C. ended his cross examination. Mr Black realized that some damage had been done which he wanted to correct by a re-examination to elicit from him that although no benefit was derived from the land nonetheless they were visiting it on and off and had intended one day to sell it. Hence the projected survey and division. The case for the Robuste family was closed, but the barrister reserved the right to call further evidence in rebuttal in the light of the defendant's case.

When the Court resumed the next day it was now the turn of Monsieur Jerôme to prove how he had prescribed the land. Ever since he had purchased the *chassé* he had occupied the land as his property. He had never seen any of the plaintiffs visiting it. Besides he has fenced the whole area a few years back and no one ever objected. Monsieur Jerôme gave evidence with such ease as if he was having a conversation with friends in his salon. Even in his cross examination when Mr Black suggested he had only put the fence after the visit of the surveyor he agreed. He wanted to prevent people, like the plaintiffs, from coming on the land after he had prescribed it. He insisted that he had never lied in his life and that he would not do so now at his age just for a few acres of land.

When the Court resumed for the third time the defence called the watchman of the *chassé*, to give evidence. He declared that ever since Monsieur Jerôme had become owner of the *chassé* he had been in his service as watchman and that he had never seen any of the Robuste family, not even the late Gaston, on the land. He always knew that it was part of the *chassé* and he had, as part of his duty, included the land in question in his round and had never allowed any trespasser into it. He was, he added, related to the Robuste and if one of them ever came on the land he would not have failed to notice. In cross examination the watchman maintained what he had said in examination in chief, except that he failed to describe where the plaintiffs lived in Quatre Bornes and how he was related to them.

The plaintiffs' counsel, Mr Black, who had reserved his right to call evidence in rebuttal, now invoked that right and called the surveyor in the witness box. The surveyor was a man of integrity and as a professional had built himself a sound reputation. He explained how his services were retained to make a division of a land which was described by both Jean and Paul, with a precision that indicated their familiarity with it.

The case being closed on both sides, each of the two Counsels offered his arguments, in favour of his client, stressing the legal definition of uninterrupted occupation. The Judge reserved his judgment.

A month later when judgment was delivered it was in favour of the defendant. It was based on facts as adduced by the defence, Paul's version was rejected as unreliable, the surveyor's evidence was not considered material to the issue and the occasional rounds of the watchman were accepted as conclusive proof of occupation giving rise to prescription.

The plaintiffs were dumbfounded. Even their Counsel could not believe his ears. Completely broken in spirit they returned home to live with the sad memory of their judicial misadventure. All of a sudden they were deprived of a property on which they had counted so much to be of assistance to Ernest who was already in France. They were advised against an appeal as a judgment based on facts was rarely reversed. The inhabitants of Midlands who all along had known the Robuste family as the owners, cursed the law and the system of justice.

Ernest in Paris

When the news of the Court case became official, Ernest was in Paris. He had not expected the outcome to be otherwise. He did not even mention a word about it in his letter, it was as if it had never happened. He had left Mauritius while the case was pending because he was convinced it was a waste of time to await the issue. His earnings from private tuition and a job as a teacher in a private secondary school had enabled him to pay his air fare and keep some money to face the initial difficulties.

He had left in 1971 when the economy had taken a serious down turn and young people were emigrating en masse to Australia or Europe in search of a better future. Ernest was lucky that France had not yet clamped down with a visa system to stem the tide of the Charter plane immigrants. There was a large Mauritian colony in Paris when he landed in Orly and two of his friends, with whom he was in correspondence, were kind enough to meet him at the airport to take charge of him until he could find a job. They were from Rose-Hill and he had known them from his early youth.

Ernest was taken to a poor suburb of the city where his friends had a room in an old apartment building with broken window panes and peeling paint. It was a squalid neighbourhood inhabited mainly by Africans and Arabs. As it was early morning, he could see droves of them going to catch the bus or the metro for the day's work. He felt depressed at the sight of the poverty which he had not expected to see in a city like Paris. The glossy magazines, the television pictures, the lights of the city centre, the bistros, the restaurants and the beautiful girls had created in his mind a glittering place where people were well dressed, healthy, living in comfort, without the ugly sight of the human underclass which haunts the cities of the third world.

His friends, Lochun and Pierre, had prepared a small bed for him and showed him a corner where he could put his only suitcase. After coffee they left informing him they would be back by 7 p.m. Taking his courage in both hands and giving a thought to his parents, he got down to face his destiny by first making a survey of the room to which he brought a little tidiness. After a rest, he explored the vicinity where he discovered that the garbage had not been collected, the grass had not been mown and plastic, paper and empty beer cans littered every corner. The first impression was a great disappointment and he almost regretted leaving the comfort of his home for the ugliness of his new surroundings.

There was plenty of work available for immigrants in those days provided they accepted low wages and agreed to be outside the social security system. After two days, he began to enquire about the possibility of employment. Having never scrounged, he felt embarrassed to continue taking advantage of his friends' hospitality. The room was small with hardly enough space for two people; now with his presence it was overcrowded.

It took another whole week before Lochun helped him acquire a job as a dish washer in a restaurant within walking distance of their address. It was a small, unassuming place, but clean. Its speciality was 'couscous', the favourite food of the North Africans, the main customers. After the first night as dish washer, Ernest, in his small bed, began to meditate on his destiny. What a far cry from dish washing to medicine! But the die was cast and he was not the type to look back. Dish washing was the crucible of his fortitude. He remembered that George Orwell had done the same job in Paris and Chou En Lai and Ho Chi Min had worked as mechanics at Renault. One day at the restaurant he met a young Algerian who had also come to France to do medicine but had no means. They became friends. The Algerian was working in a pharmaceutical company and he introduced Ernest to the boss who was so impressed that he gave him a job in the store with a decent salary.

His knowledge of chemistry helped him in his work and within a few months he was given a promotion and security in his employment. Ernest was now in a position to rent a room of his own in a better area and make some savings. His new surroundings put him in a better mood to explore Paris and discover the beauty of the city. Abbas, the Algerian friend, who used to see him every day for a coffee or a meal, one day announced the good news that he was going to Montpellier where he had been admitted to the Faculty of Medicine. Thanks to a close contact in the government, he had been awarded a scholarship by the French Cooperation. When Abbas left Ernest felt a sudden void although his circle of friends kept enlarging. Among the immigrants from other countries, he met several young men with brilliant qualifications who, like him, had come to Paris to try to benefit from opportunities of higher studies.

One day, he was surprised to receive a letter from Abbas inviting him to Montpellier to visit the Faculty of Medicine and become acquainted with the procedure for admission and the programme of studies. Abbas even undertook to accommodate him for a few days. It was an opportunity he did not wish to miss. He took the train to Marseilles and arrived at his friend's lodging in the Student Residence. With the savings he had made, he could live for 9 months, just the time needed to complete the first year. He liked to gamble and it was the second time he decided to take a plunge into the hazards of uncertainty, the first time was when he left Mauritius. He thus gave up his Paris job and applied for admission which was not difficult to obtain. Abbas, in his generosity, put him up free of charge the first year. He was told that if his results were good he would be kept on the degree course, otherwise he would be eliminated. Only the best students made it to the second year.

Ernest's results were so good that, in addition to a place in the second year, he was awarded a stipend that assured him of his board and lodging for the duration of the course.

Montpellier

The six years of medical studies did not seem to last long. Ernest was in his element and applied to his studies with a determination not only to pass his examination but to score the highest marks. Obsessed by his background and the disadvantage of his birth, he wanted to make up for these handicaps by a performance to give him an edge over others, especially those Mauritian students with an uppish attitude. His status as a holder of a French scholarship was in itself deserving of a consideration above those privately financed. His hard work and his intelligence earned him the high esteem of his professors. At the end of his studies when he qualified for his medical degree, the board of examiners were so impressed by his work, that they unanimously recommended him for a specialisation. After another three years, he finished his course with a degree in Urology with specialisation in transplant surgery. He accepted an appointment as Registrar Specialist at his hospital.

His success gave great prestige not only to Ernest but to his country of origin, Mauritius, as well. The other Mauritian students of the Faculty of Medicine felt proud of him and shared in his success. Ernest, now Dr Ernest Robuste, did not wish to spend the rest of his life in Montpellier. He had not forgotten his parents and his house in Quatre Bornes where he had grown up, his childhood friends, his own humble origin and his people who were living on the margin of society. He had a duty towards them and he planned to return to his roots, where he felt he really belonged. But before returning home, he wanted to acquire some more experience in a different medical environment. The best place was London. He easily obtained a position as Urologist in one of the most prestigious hospitals: Charing Cross Hospital.

Dr Ernest Robuste in London

In London, Ernest felt more at home than in Montpellier. In this vast metropolis, he found opportunities for a cultural life which he had to sacrifice for the sake of his studies. He also made many friends among Mauritians who were now eager for his company. His skill as a surgeon on kidney transplant became so well known that he was entrusted with complicated cases.

Urology was a branch of medicine which had not made sufficient headway in Mauritius. Difficult cases were sent to South Africa to be operated. The kidney machine for dialysis had not even been introduced. Dr Ernest thought he could be of some use to his countrymen and could persuade the government to provide facilities for the treatment of such cases. After a year at Charing Cross Hospital, he took three months' leave and flew to Mauritius.

His reputation had preceded him and the newspapers which had been following his career gave wide publicity to his success. From the tone of the press report, Dr Ernest Robuste had been socially promoted and assimilated into the high society of Rose-Hill and Beau Bassin. There was no talk about his grandfather Gaston, or his father the cabinet maker. Dr Ernest had been detached from his past and re-invented as a member of the intellectual aristocracy.

When the aircraft was about to land, he was surprised to hear the announcement that friends were waiting for him at the VIP Lounge. Indeed, when the door opened, he was among the first passengers to leave the aircraft, although he was travelling economy. When he saw the airport official who had come to meet him taking a direction away from the gate of arriving passengers, he told him that his parents were waiting for him and he would rather go through the normal channel. His doctor friends who had arranged for the VIP welcome felt obliged to come to the Immigration desk to greet him.

Having not seen his father and mother and the other members of the family for at least twelve years, he threw himself into their arms amid tears of joy. He thanked his doctor friends for the transport they had provided but preferred to travel in the taxi with his parents. He learnt that his friends, whom he had known in Montpellier and London, wanted to receive him with the dignity due to his reputation and had arranged for the VIP treatment. Dr Ernest Robuste thanked them for their attention and promised to see them at some later date.

It was with deep emotion that he set foot in his Quatre Bornes house. The place had not changed. The garden was the same except somewhat overgrown. The fruit trees had withstood cyclone Gervaise and were in good health, the mango trees already bearing little mangoes. His brother and sister had grown into young adults and the parents and uncles and aunts had aged a bit, but were still hale and hearty. He was glad to see everyone as he had left them. This enabled him to take up the thread without feeling the effect of the long break occasioned by his absence. The more he looked around to bring back the memories of the past the happier he felt. Neighbours, relatives and friends came to welcome and congratulate him for his brilliant achievements. The press did not give him any respite, the journalists were at his heels and had followed him to his residence.

The first week was spent in receiving and paying visits. One of his first duties was to meet the parents of his two benefactors, Lochun and Pierre, and express his gratitude and promised them that he was at their service for any medical problem should the need ever arise. Afterwards he registered himself as a medical practitioner at the Ministry of Health where he was received by the Minister. The latter was keen on recruiting him as a specialist with the privilege of private practice.

After the usual formalities, he assumed duty at Victoria Hospital the following week and in the meantime informed

Charing Cross of his resignation. After spending a month with his parents, he moved into a small flat in Curepipe where he could be more easily accessible. The private clinics enlisted his services thanks to his medical friends. Kidney cases were not as common as cardiac ones, with the result that he was not much in demand in the beginning. He thought that if he were to be useful, he must have the equipment to operate. He tried to persuade the government to buy a machine for dialysis and equipment to facilitate kidney transplants.

While he was engaged in looking after minor cases, one of his friends, himself a well known surgeon, asked him to see a young patient in a clinic in Floreal. The young man had an acute kidney problem and his advice was solicited. It was an advanced case of kidney failure which necessitated a transplant; a donor had to be found without delay, preferably a donor in the family to avoid rejection after the transplant. The alternative was to send him to Europe, London or France, for the operation. It was known that the doctor had successfully carried out transplant cases in London and Montpellier. The patient was advised that the operation could comfortably be carried out in Mauritius with success rated at 85%.

The young patient was Donald, and he happened to be the paternal grandson of Monsieur Jerôme; the doctor advised Donald's parents that he had full confidence in the competence of the surgeon Ernest Robuste who could be entrusted with the operation because, from his experience, they could not obtain a better specialist in Europe. After much hesitation and family consultation Donald's father gave his consent. The frizzy hair of Dr E. Robuste still carried an element of prejudice in certain circles.

The parents of young Donald were becoming anxious as the fateful day approached, but for the medical profession it was a *grande première*. It was the first time that a kidney transplant was being undertaken in Mauritius and several practitioners had expressed keen interest. Some even volunteered to assist to have an opportunity to witness the procedure.

The operation took several hours, prolonging the agonising suspense as time ticked away. At long last a nurse appeared to announce that the operation was over and the patient was stable. It was only when Dr Robuste came out of the operating theatre looking relaxed that the parents and relatives felt relieved. He told them that Donald needed complete rest and that he was still under sedation. It would take a month before he could go home because he had to be under constant observation to make sure that there was no rejection. He allowed the father, the mother and the grandfather to see him for a few minutes.

The grandfather to whom Donald was the apple of his eye and who was day and night at the clinic until his discharge, wanted to pay his respects to the doctor and thank him personally for the new life given to his grandson. It was only when he heard his name that an old memory was triggered. He was now sure that the surgeon belonged to the same family with whom he had had litigation about lands in the Midlands.

The Trust Fund

Monsieur Jerôme felt guilty and suddenly realised the futility of wealth and power after the agonising experience of his grandson's illness. He remembered how he had prescribed the Midlands land under false pretences thus depriving the young Ernest of the means to pay for his studies. He swallowed whatever pride was still left and met the doctor at the clinic. In a very humble voice, he thanked him for saving the life of his grandson, and added that he had come to him to express his regret for the harm done to his family by prescribing their lands. He was feeling so humble in his presence that he had come to discuss the manner in which he could make amends. He was offering not only to return the land but also double the acreage as compensation for the damage done.

Dr Ernest Robuste looked at him and addressed the following words:

'*When I operated upon your grandson, I did not know who he was. For me he was a human being who needed treatment. I am happy that he can now be cured. The Midlands case had been out of my mind even before I left for France. The struggle I had to face to complete my studies strengthened my resolve to stand on my own feet. The loss of the land was a blessing in disguise. I am no longer interested in it and nor are my parents. The night vigil I started in France is over. My mission now is to bring light to those still in darkness, either through ignorance or poverty. Perhaps you could help by setting up a trust fund to help deserving students of poor background to pursue higher studies*'.

M. Jerôme, who felt quite overwhelmed by such a reaction, gave his agreement and suggested that the surgeon should agree to give his name to the trust. Dr E. Robuste told him he was moved by his attention but would prefer to give it the name of his grandfather Gaston, as a tribute to a memory which had sustained him in all his tribulations.

The story ends here, but the Fund continues.

The Temple in the Sea.

An old Church in a remote village.

A modern mosque.

The gate of the Central Market, Port Louis.

~ The Temple in the Sea ~

His name was Lall Ganawa but he was known in his village and by his friends as Lall, Lall of Poste de Flacq. He was very popular, thanks to his kindheartedness and ability to make friends with the high and the low, the rich and the poor, the powerful and the weak. He had a modest education but he radiated a warmth and a sincerity which endeared him to anyone whom he came across.

One day he came to see me at my residence in Bancilhon Street, Port Louis. It must have been in the mid-seventies. I had met him before and knew about his background. He came with a few friends and informed me that they were from the village of Laventure. He greeted me as *mamoo*, a maternal uncle, yet he did not look younger than me. *Mamoo* and *chacha* are terms of respect and people in our society accept them as such, not necessarily in the sense of blood relationship. As there were half a dozen of them, I suspected they had come on a special mission, the success of which depended on my support. Lall told me that it was their ambition to build a temple and my help was badly needed. I asked him in what way I could help for the realization of their project. It was then that they revealed the true purpose of their visit. The temple was to be built on an island which was government property and my intervention was important for the lease of the site.

The island in question, or islet to be precise, is one of several, dotting the lagoon of Poste de Flacq, a fishing village. The islets are heaps of boulders projecting above the sea and looking like freaks of nature sitting oddly in the water. There was little vegetation on them, each islet could not consist of more than one to two acres. I could not understand how they came into existence and why the sea did not cover them. Be that as it may. The question was that I was intrigued by the idea and wanted to see the place. How could a temple be built on such a small area in the sea?

Poste de Flacq, especially that part of it where Lall had recently established domicile and opened a shop, is a picturesque fishing village. Part of the lagoon is covered with mangroves and the islets give the whole place a quaint aspect. Across the narrow arm of the sea one has a clear view of St Geran Hotel with its beaches planted with filaos and coconut palms. There had been diversified activities in Poste de Flacq at one time and the abandoned lime kiln was a reminder. Not far from the fishing post there is a Catholic Church and small concrete whitewashed houses with well tended flower gardens and bougainvilleas creeping over the walls. The fishing boats were moored in what used to be a fish landing station. Close by, in an open space under a pipal tree, fishermen gather for a game of cards or dominoes over a bottle of beer from Lall's shop. Lall was liberal with credit sales when their catch was poor but he used to recover his money during the good days, because fishermen as a rule are good customers and conscious of the necessity of maintaining an honest relationship with their local shopkeeper.

The fishermen were living in relatively comfortable conditions. Each had a house and a family. They were regular church-goers, although after the Sunday service they would make their customary call at the local shop for their tot of rum. Some of them were earning good money by hiring their boats to tourists whom they would take out for a day's fishing. The St Geran Hotel and the other hotels across the arm of the sea were supplying them with good business. Tourism had changed their life style by bringing extra earnings. They had refrigerators and colour TV, a few also had an additional source of income from remittances by offspring who had migrated to the United Kingdom or France. So, life was easy and the inhabitants, irrespective of their ethnic origin, were living as members of a large family. The fishermen who were of Afro origin and the others of Indian stock used to socialise without any inhibition. There was a solidarity among them because they belonged to the same village.

Jacques, a young fisherman, who was a staunch follower of Gaetan Duval[1], had gained, with the passage of time, an importance above his station. He had become in a way leader of the village fishermen as it was generally accepted his political connection could get things done. The members of the Assembly paid court to him for his cooperation in organizing private meetings. There was political division among the fishermen too. Some were pro-PMSD[2] and others pro-MMM[3]. Very few among them were Labour. But the few together with the PMSD counted and that explains the standing of Jacques as a local political celebrity.

I arranged to visit the site where it had been decided to construct the temple. My visit had already received advance publicity because Lall had announced the date and the purpose. A small group had greeted my arrival, Jacques had also joined in. We had to cross the sea because as the islet was a few hundred feet from the mainland, I had either to ford it or be ferried on the back of one of the volunteers. I chose to wade through barefoot. Once on the islet, I was shown the site where the temple was to be constructed and also the space for a hall to receive devotees. I noticed that some of the boulders had been levelled by filling the gaps with small stones. Its use as a retreat by Lall and his friends raised my suspicion that they met to smoke cannabis i.e. ganja.

1. Gaëtan Duval: a colourful but highly successful local politician, leader of the Parti Mauricien Social Démocrate, who died in 1996.
2. PMSD: Parti Mauricien Social Démocrate.
3. MMM: Movement Militant Mauricien.

The mischievous smile on Lall's face confirmed it. He was, however, sincere in his desire to build a temple dedicated to Shivji, the supreme deity in the Hindu pantheon, and he was prepared for any sacrifice to attain his objective. I was in a quandary. I knew that Lall was not only a ganja or marijuana addict, but also a cultivator. In those days the law was not so severe as today because ganja, although illegal, was not a menace to our youth and to society. Brown sugar and heroin had not yet invaded our territory. Besides, ganja had a significance with a religious undertone, Hindus used to smoke the leaves and drink the bhang, a ganja brew, on the occasion of Holi as part of their culture. In the early days of Indian immigration, the British authorities had even legalised the smoking by licensing ganja shops, known to the Indians as 'Ganja Dokhans'. So ganja, as a drug was not so severely frowned upon. But later it was made illegal to grow, sell and smoke it. On conviction the penalty could be imprisonment, but there was no confiscation of property of those found guilty of trafficking. I have always taken a lenient view of ganja smoking because I know it is not as harmful as is pretended. Besides, the cultural aspect cannot be overlooked. Its deleterious impact should not be exaggerated. So for me, the fact that Lall might be tempted to use the place for occasional ganja session did not detract from encouraging him in his endeavour to build the temple.

My encouragement was like a green light to Lall and his friends. They assumed that no obstacle could be placed on their path now that I had given my blessing. I felt a bit uneasy because the islet was government property and without a lease any building could be pulled down as being illegal. I knew that even if I made a strong case, the procedure would be long before approval could be given. There would be a survey for the assessment of the rental value and the feelings of the non-Hindu inhabitants as to the siting of the temple would have to be taken on board. I realized that even when all the hurdles mentioned above could be overcome, there might still be ministerial objection in the Cabinet. Some might come up with the bright idea that something else than a temple would be more appropriate. There would be delaying tactics. We live in a multi-religious society and the lease of a small islet for a temple could give rise to similar demands by other religious groups on other islets. It could assume a political dimension and the absence of a consensus in Cabinet might scupper the whole project. I took time for further thought and I informed Lall and his friends that they should have patience and not remove a single stone until I gave the signal. But they were impatient and in a hurry to lay the foundation. They told me that so long as they had my support, they could not care about anything else. I persuaded them nonetheless to wait for a few weeks.

I did not mention the project to any of my colleagues in the Cabinet. After anxious consideration, I just decided to give them the go-ahead. I came to the conclusion that once a start was made and the place converted into a place of worship, no one would dare to interfere, because of strong religious sensibilities, and no authority would do anything to stand in the way.

Lall had the advantage of having the local inhabitants on his side. He had the reputation of a great benefactor and a man of strong religious beliefs. He used to organise functions at which he would invite all the locals and treat them with lavish hospitality. At one of those functions known as 'Katha', and to which I was invited, I was amused to see the presence of a few small time dealers in ganja. One from Port Louis was busy serving food as if he belonged to the organising committee. I immediately realized that all these friends of Lall belonged to the brotherhood of cannabis with a bond too strong to break. Whatever the turn of fortune, they would stick together and there was no room in their relationship for betrayal.

When I gave Lall the green light to start the construction of the temple, the whole village promised its cooperation. Strengthened by such solidarity, he organised the ceremony of the laying of the foundation stone to be performed by me. It was raining, I remember, and not many people had turned up for the occasion, apart from his close relations and friends. I was told later that many people did not believe that the project could materialize. The ground could not be levelled as it was full of boulders. Tons of macadam were needed to fill the gaps for a level surface, but the boulders provided a solid foundation and with the addition of cement and macadam, a strong structure was not difficult to put up.

Once the foundation stone was laid, the burden fell upon Lall to raise funds for the construction. As very few people had faith in a temple in the sea on a heap of boulders the task was a most daunting and a challenging one. Lall set upon it with the determination of a man obsessed. His finance had only one source, ganja. He was already an expert in the cultivation and had his network to dispose of the crop. He unhesitatingly got down to business and enlisted the cooperation of the local planters to earmark certain fields for his use. He also tried to hedge himself against any possible betrayal by befriending certain police officers. He thus reaped a large benefit which he devoted to the purchase of materials. The structure was raised and the temple began to take shape, but there was a long way to go and donations either in cash or in kind were not forthcoming. Nonetheless Lall was not daunted, he soldiered on. Luck, however, was not always on his side. In the illegal business of ganja cultivation several risks were involved. Besides the possibility of being betrayed by whistle blowers, the destruction by rivals or loss by theft was forever present.

One day Lall disappeared from circulation, he had been caught red handed on his ganja plantation, convicted and sentenced to gaol. The temple's construction was suspended. The structure was there and his friends continued to mark their presence, often for a smoking session but that was all. The authorities closed their eyes. Any interference or notice to stop the work could provoke the wrath of the inhabitants. There was no doubt that without ganja money no progress could be registered. One fine morning, Lall reappeared at my residence in Port Louis. He was in high spirits, the temporary absence had not affected his morale at all, he was accustomed to such breaks. If anything, he was a beneficiary, having had time to meditate within the four walls of his cell and renew acquaintances with members of the Ganja fraternity to run errands for him. Errand boys were indispensable for his network to deliver the precious stuff. Lall talked to me about a katha and resumption of work at the temple to which he had given the name of Shiv Sagar Mandir. His friends also were in a better frame of mind, being now sure that something would happen as Lall had the ability to find the resources for the temple. He even sold two acres of his own land to meet urgent commitments. When the temple took real shape, people were attracted to visit it. Even politicians saw in the project potential for political mileage. They made regular visits and promised their contribution. As a good opportunist, Lall took full advantage of their offer of assistance. He thus managed to get the Development Works Corporation to fill a portion of the sea thereby giving access to the temple so that the road could be extended and the islet linked to the mainland. Lorry loads of macadam to level the ground were provided free. In the course of a few months, the boulders were completely covered and a few shrines to house the deities saw the light. The dome of the temple with the lotus on top was finally completed. Lall organised a large katha to inaugurate the temple, although partly incomplete. He had to do it because it was the only way he could publicise his achievement and induce people to make donations. The device worked. It is the inherent characteristic of people to make appearances only in the final phase of the completion of any painstaking and expensive undertaking demanding hard sacrifice. Everybody wanted to share in the glory of the work in its final phase although few had made any effort to lend support at the initial stage when hard labour was required. Many candidates came forward to take the driving seat and raise the standard of victory and consign Lall to a back stage role. Fortunately they did not succeed because local opinion was against them.

By now the temple had become a jewel of Poste de Flacq. Raising its cupola proudly from the sea it became a centre of attraction to visitors from across the four corners of the mainland. Even those who were not religiously inspired had to admit that the temple moved them to the belief of the existence of a superior divine power. Lall by himself could not have achieved what he did without that driving force, which only comes from the Superior Being. He began to be reincarnated as a man fired by divine touch and this elevated his standing among those who knew him.

Lall was running his shop with the help of his two sons but he was spending most of his time at the temple in the company of friends who praised his achievements in glowing terms. Time was flowing in blissful leisure and Lall looked the happiest of mortals.

I had in the meantime lost office and, although our relationship continued steadfast, we met less often. Ministers of the new government were paying regular visits to the temple and their presence gave an aura of respectability to the place and discouraged the authorities from prying too closely into activities, as distinct from the purely religious ones. All the deities had been installed, each in his niche, and the priest had given his blessing by injecting life into them. Worshippers began to flock by bus loads from all over the country. Most of them also took advantage of the ideal setting for a picnic. Of course, the food was strictly vegetarian composed of offerings and no alcohol was permitted. To observe the sanctity of the temple, the prohibition had been extended to cover not only the island but the close vicinity on the mainland. Even the non-Hindus venerated the sacredness of the place and observed the rule.

I had not seen Lall for some time, I thought he had become a recluse. Men of his temperament harbour a desire for total renunciation as their wisdom matures with the years. But Lall was not enjoying good health. One day I received a telephone call announcing his death. I was shocked but then thought that he had completed his mission and his death was a crowning conclusion of a life marked by such deep love for his faith. I attended the cremation not very far from the temple by the side of the road leading to it. The gathering of friends and relatives to pay the last respect was quite impressive. All those in high position who had known him were present; everybody paid compliment to the rich legacy he was leaving behind. It was a fitting tribute to cremate him in a place where his memory would always be associated with the temple to which he had devoted so much labour and wealth. Any worshipper, passing by, to pray to the gods and solicit their blessings, would inevitably first be reminded of the man of humble condition who made such religious pilgrimages possible and brought his fellow brothers a step closer to their Creator.

I went back to Poste de Flacq after an absence of two years. The temple was resplendent in its whiteness with sea water lapping against the shoreline. Two busloads of worshippers were performing their pooja[4]. Barefooted tourists were taking photos of the deities. The atmosphere was calm in spite of the presence of the crowd. Not a voice was heard. A divine presence seemed to pervade the whole environment. I thought of Lall and his dream. I also felt elevated in spirit and a blissful peace descended upon me. I felt moved by the memory of courage and devotion of a man,

4. pooja: religious ceremony.

ignorant of the scriptures, but believing in the power of his God, Shivji, a belief which spurred him to defy all odds to make of his dream a reality. To people not acquainted with the full story of Lall, he will remain unwept and unsung, but to those intimately connected with him, he has left the memory of a benefactor, a deeply religious man, a great devotee of Shivji and the architect of a rare monument, a temple in the sea.

I met Jacques, the faithful Jacques, and the sons of Lall in the village. Jacques had not changed. It was a Sunday afternoon and he could not be expected to be sober, but he was full of life and proclaiming to all the inhabitants my presence in the village. He still retained some importance but had lost his old influence. He was respected but not listened to.

Lall had ten children in all; six sons and four daughters, a robust performance to guarantee the continuation of the dynasty till kingdom come. Out of the six sons, one had the face of a grandfather, two looked still young, others were sporting a greying moustache. The sons had their houses in the village and gave the impression of a closely knit family. We talked about the old days and the Temple. They told me that the administration was in the family with the cooperation of other members.

Lall himself was born in Laventure, a village a few miles away. He belonged to the Gunawas, even in those days, a large family sufficient to fill half of Laventure. With his contribution, and now that of his ten children, the tribe had grown considerably in size, having to overspill in Poste de Flacq.

I loved my visit to Poste de Flacq. It permitted me to renew my connection with the village, meet the people and above all to see the temple and pay my respects to the memory of my friend Lall.

MAURITIUS THROUGH THE LOOKING GLASS:
A COLLECTION OF SHORT STORIES

Jacob Adrianus Wildschut
Rose Hill, Mauritius
9 June 2003